The Last Prom

Miles Cornelius

Published by Miles Cornelius, 2024.

The Last Prom: A Misty Night Story
Miles Cornelius

Cornelius Publishing

THE LAST PROM

First edition. October 7, 2024.

ISBN: 979-8227290410

Written by Miles Cornelius.

Also by Miles Cornelius

Blood City: A Misty Night Story
The Black Forest
Yellow Gloves: A Misty Night Story
The Last Prom
Hellmervick

Table of Contents

I would like to dedicate this book to my sister's DeAnna, Virginia, and Judy.

I would also like to dedicate this book to the P{orterville High School graduating class of 1986.

June 1967

The hour was midnight and the sleepy town of Sotterville was enveloped in darkness. Streetlights illuminated the darkness, casting light and shadows upon the buildings that lined the main street of town. The hospital was no exception. With only a few lights beaming down from open windows, it was shrouded in stillness. Off in the distance, a siren could be heard and as it approached the hospital, the red lights lit up the emergency room doors. Two paramedics jetted from the front seat of the ambulance, moving quickly to the back, they opened the doors while another paramedic from the back of the ambulance quickly helped to remove the stretcher from within. The emergency room doors swooshed open as bright fluorescent light filled the void between the hospital and the ambulance. As the paramedics rushed to bring the woman on the stretcher inside, they were met by the residing physician. "What do you have?" the Doctor asked. "Heavy labor, the husband is on the way, for some reason he refused to ride with us." A nurse met them as they entered the hospital. "Put her in room one," the doctor said, "give her 2 ccs of Morphine and prep her for delivery." As they entered the room the woman began to scream. The doctor looked over at the nurse, "Where is that Morphine Nurse?" The nurse quickly moved over to a small cabinet and opened the top drawer. She removed a needle and a small bottle. She looked at the label to make sure it was the drug she needed. She hurried as fast as she could, plunging the needle into the bottle, she held it up and pulled back the plunger. As she walked over to the woman, she noticed that her stomach was larger than normal, and seemed to move, the woman screamed again. The doctor removed the woman's nightgown as he strapped her legs into two stirrups that were on the edge of the bed. The woman screamed again as the nurse plunged the needle into her thigh. She stepped back in horror as the woman's stomach moved again, this time she saw what looked like the imprint of a tiny face on the woman's skin. "I have never seen anything like that doctor." the nurse said. The doctor looked at her and back at the woman's stomach. "Get around there and hold her hand." he looked at the woman in labor, "Okay ma'am, I am going to need you to push." The woman shook her head as the nurse took her hand. She screamed again as her stomach looked as if it was being pushed out from the inside. The doctor took a step back. "We are going to have to do a cesarean delivery, nurse, get the anesthesiologist down here right now." The nurse moved away from the screaming woman, keeping her eyes on the stomach as it moved back and forth, like the baby inside was trying to claw its way out of her womb. The doctor tried to calm the woman down, "Ma'am, we are going to have to do a cesarean on you to help bring your beautiful baby into the world." he smiled, but the woman did not hear him. She felt as if her insides were being ripped apart, she screamed again as a stream of blood trickled from her mouth then she passed out.

1

Tragedy strikes in many ways and at different times. It can happen anywhere, and it can come from many sources. There are many tragic events that have happened to the human race over the centuries. From buildings burning, earthquakes, icebergs, tornadoes, and hurricanes. These events have caused the deaths of many human lives. But no tragedy on the planet is worse than those that have been caused by human hands. This is the tragic story that befell the students and faculty of Sotterville High School in California in 1984. Sotterville is a town of about ninety thousand people nestled in the San Juan King valley in central California. During the summer months, the temperatures can sit in the high nineties and even upwards towards a hundred degrees. Our story takes place during one of the hottest summers Sotterville ever encountered. Monday morning, June 1st to be specific, the week of senior prom. The day was just like any other day, birds were singing, the sun was bright, and it was already ninety-eight degrees outside. Homer looked over at his alarm clock, it read seven and he couldn't wait to get this day started. He was excited about going to the prom this year, it would be his first time to ever go to a dance. He had always been a shy boy who had trouble making friends. It was not always this way, when he was younger, everyone seemed to like him. From first grade through fourth grade, he had lots of friends and the occasional girlfriend. But something seemed to change for Homer after that. Over that summer between fourth and fifth grades, he began to change. He became more reclusive as he wanted to focus on learning. He started reading more and really getting into what was being taught at school. That was when his troubles really started. People that used to be his friends began calling him names, like nerd, or geek. As he got older, it seemed to get worse. Soon, he was being picked on every day. He did his best to stay away from everyone at school, but it was hard to avoid them. BY the time he was in high school, most of the bullying stopped, but there were those who really thought they were better than everyone else that still liked to try and push him around. Of course, by now, he really did not care. He had a few friends that he hung around with. Mark, Todd, Steven, they were like him and they were his friends. Then there was Sara, she was a special friend. But not anyone he would date, he did not date at all. He had always wanted to go on a date, and all through high school he never even had a girlfriend. This was one of things that he had picked on for. He had been called gay, but he knew he was not. He liked girls; he was just too shy to ever ask them out. But now that he was a senior and high school was almost over, he would be going to college. He always felt that once he went to college, he would find the girl of his dreams. He knew she was out there, and he knew that once he found her, he would be her whole world. He was laying in bed thinking about how this would be his last week in high school and how great it was going to be. His alarm clock sounded, just like it did every day, only today he felt like it sounded cheerier. He reached over and shut it off, like he always did, but it felt like more a triumph than anything else. He yawned and stretched as he rose from his bed. He smoothed out his dark brown hair and made sure it was out of his eyes. He was wearing red and white striped pajamas, and as he rolled out of bed, he smoothed the pant legs out. He hated it when they rolled up on his legs while he was sleeping. He wanted to just sleep in his underwear, but that would be inappropriate, and his mother would make him put on the pajamas anyway. He took them off and threw them on the bed, walked over to a mirror he had on the back of his bedroom door, and looked at himself in his underwear. He stood five feet nine inches and weighed about 120 pounds. He felt like he was in good physical shape, but also, he felt weak because he never worked out. He raised his right arm and flexed his muscle, too small he thought. He slipped out of his underwear and looked at his naked body in the mirror. He frowned at himself, there was no wonder he could never fit in with the jocks at school, and it was no wonder they made fun of him so much. He turned in disgust and walked into the bathroom that was adjoined to his room. Her always felt special that he had his own bathroom, he felt like he had more privacy this way. He turned on his shower and when he felt the water was warm, he stepped in. He loved the feeling of a hot shower first thing in the morning, it made him feel clean. When he was finished, he stepped out and dried himself off. With the towel wrapped around, he went back into his bedroom and proceeded to get dressed. He put on a pair of jeans and a plain black T-shirt. As he tied his shoes, the thought about the prom, he was going to ask Racheal to the prom. He shook his head; she is too pretty and would most likely say no. He has had a crush on her since the third grade, but he knew she would just laugh at him if he asked her, so he put that thought out of his head. Then he thought about a couple of girls he knew, but they would just laugh too. He was going to have to go to the prom by himself. He was okay with that though; it would be cheaper and maybe he would be able to pick up a girl there. He glanced over at his clock, it was almost a quarter to eight, no time for breakfast, he would need to get his ass to the bus stop so he didn't miss it. This was the part of the day he liked the least. There were a couple of guys that rode the same bus as him, and they always picked on him. One of these days he was not going to put up with any longer, he would just snap and put an end to the endless torture he faced. Regardless, he grabbed his backpack and headed out the door.

He did not stop and make time for breakfast before he left his house. He knew that it would only slow him down and he really wanted to get to school. He only lived two blocks from the bus stop, so it did not take him very long to walk there. He walked down the street thinking about the prom and how much fun he was going to have. He had not gone to any of them before, and this would be his first one, and he was super excited about it. As he approached the bus stop, he saw Doug and Jerry, they were standing there with Sara, they were always with her. She was a vision of beauty. Standing five feet eight inches, long blonde hair, two eyes that were perfect blue, like two shallow ponds with the sun shining on them. Doug and Jerry, who were both jocks. Doug was the quarterback of the football team, why he didn't have his own car, Homer never knew. Jerry was on the basketball team and played center, he was not as mean as Doug, but he played off of Doug's rude comments, and to Homer, that made him just as bad. Doug seemed to feel he was better than everyone else and acted that way too. Jerry was Sara's boyfriend, and that was why he was with her. Sometimes he would actually be nice to him, and Sara was always nice to him. He admired that about her. The bus stop was on the corner in front of a small neighborhood market, even though they sold very little groceries, they still called it a market. As Homer approached, Doug took notice of him. "Look, here comes Homo." The other people standing around the bus stop laughed, except for Doug and Sara. "Why don't you leave him alone this morning?" Sara said, poking Doug in the arm. Doug looked at her and smirked, "Why? Someone needs to keep him in line." As Homer got closer, Jerry waved and said hello. Homer waved back and smiled. "Oh look," Doug said, "He must have a crush on you Jerry, better look out!" Homer ignored this comment and walked over to Sara. He smiled as he said good morning to her, and Sara smiled back. "Are you going to the prom, Homer?" she asked. Homer smiled; it was the first time she had asked him about this. "Yes, I am, I can't wait for it, I finally am going to get to go." "Do you have someone that you want to go with?" Homer blushed and looked around, but before he could answer Doug spoke up. "Yes, if he had a brother, he would probably go with him, but since he doesn't, he will have to go all by himself." Homer's face turned red with anger, and he looked at Doug. "Wow, you got some attitude going one, well come on, what you got?" Homer started to walk over to him. Doug balled his right hand into a fist. Before Homer could reach Doug, Jerry put his hand on his shoulder and stopped him. Homer looked at him sharply and Jerry shook his head no. "He will hurt you." Jerry said. "Oh, come Jerry, let the little shit come on over here, I have been waiting to show him a good time." "Shut up Doug, leave him alone alright." Doug was getting ready to meet Homer halfway when the bus pulled up and the doors swung open. Doug looked at Jerry, then back at Homer. "Next time, twerp." As they were getting on the bus, Doug waited to be last behind Homer, and when Homer was about to step on the bus, Doug pushed him. He fell and hit his chin on the second step of the bus. The bus driver looked over at Homer on the floor. "You alright kid?" he asked. Homer stood up and dusted himself off, "Yeah, I think so." The bus driver shook his head and Homer took a seat just behind the driver. As Doug got onto the bus the driver shot him a look. Doug just smiled at him and then looked the bus over as if he was looking for someone specific. He noticed that Jerry and Sara were sitting together just opposite of Homer. The seat behind Homer was empty, and Doug sat there. The driver closed the doors, checked for traffic, and when he saw it was clear, he drove off.

Doug looked around the bus again as if he was looking for someone specific, then he saw him. Two rows behind him sat another person from the football team. His name was John, and he and Doug were really good friends. John caught his eye and shook his head. Then he watched to make sure the bus driver was not paying attention and he stood up. He jetted out of his seat and quickly sat next to Doug. He was smaller than Doug and only stood about five foot four. "Did you bring it?" Doug asked. John pulled something from his pants pocket and handed something to him. "I had to steal it from the old man this morning, man is he going to shit bricks when he finds out it is gone." Doug took it from him and looked at it. It was a small can of shaving cream. Doug looked around the bus again to make sure no one was paying any attention. He shook it up a little then placed it over Homer's head. When he felt no one was looking, he began to squirt it all over Homer. "What the hell?" Homer said and put his hand in his hair. He could feel the shaving cream on his head and his neck. He stood up from his seat and turned towards Doug, who had thrown the can into the seat behind him. Homer raised his right hand and slapped at Doug, missing him completely. Doug stood up and balled his right hand into a fist, hitting Homer square in the jaw. Homer fell backwards back into the seat. The bus driver, now aware of the situation yelled, "You two sit your asses down or I will put both of you off right now." Doug and Homer both sat back down. Homer tried to clean the mess out of his hair while he was rubbing his jaw. Sara, who had been watching, pulled a napkin from her purse and offered it to Homer. He smiled at her as he took it, then he continued to clean his head and face. The bus pulled up to the school parking lot and the driver opened the doors. Everyone on the bus stood up and got in line to get off. The bus driver looked over at Doug, "You ain't going nowhere young man." Doug gave him a dirty look, "What the hell are you talking about, old man?" "You and I are going to go see Mr. Payne." Doug laughed, "I am not going to go see the principle with you, asshole." The driver stood up. He towered over Doug standing at least six foot six. He was broad shouldered and made Doug look like a dwarf. "You heard me, we are going to see the principle." "What about him?" Doug pointed at Homer who was just stepping off the bus. "Oh, him, well no, just you and I." He took Doug by the shirt collar. Doug tried to resist, but the driver had hands like a vice grip. Doug tried to shake loose, but it made the driver grasped even harder, and Doug could not resist. As they exited the bus, Doug looked over at Homer, who was standing with Sara. "You are dead meat, asshole, I will get you for this!" "Come one." said the driver as he dragged him away. Homer looked over at Sara, then he walked away. Jerry took Sara's hand and then kissed her on the cheek. "You know what I don't understand?" Jerry said, "Why do you always defend that idiot?" Sara looked at him sharply, "Who, Homer?" she asked. "Yes, I mean, he is not that bad of a person, but come on, he is really a dork." She gave him a look like she wanted to rip his guts out. He looked back at her in surprise. "Do you have a crush on him?" She smacked his arm, "mm, no. " she quipped. Then she turned her attention back to Homer as he walked away, and she smiled slightly.

Doug sat across from the principal, he hated being here, but he hated that twerp even worse. He was thinking to himself how he was going to get even with that asshole for getting him into trouble. "Listen Doug, this is the third time you have done something like this, and I hate to do it, but you will be suspended." Doug looked at him, "Are you kidding me!" He yelled as he began to stand up. "Sit your ass down, Doug! You will not talk to me like that, you can consider yourself suspended, and if you were going to go to the prom, you can kiss that goodbye." Doug's face turned a bright red. "You can't do that." he yelled. "Yes, I can, and while I am on the phone talking it over with your parents, you can sit in the office out there till they get here to pick you up." "But I graduate next week, you can't just suspend me." Mr. Payne stood up and walked around his desk. "Actually, I can. You should have known better than to pull these stunts, three times in the past two weeks, you should be smarter than that. Now get out of my office." Doug stood up, when he did, he balled his hands into a fist. Mr. Payne saw this, "I would calm yourself down, you have no one to blame but yourself." He opened the door and Doug walked out. He shook his head and sat back down at his desk, picking up the phone, he dialed the front desk. "Hello, Darla, can you please call out to Doug Burton's parents and let them know he has been suspended and they should come pick him up right now. I will fill out the paperwork and get it into his file." With that, he hung up the phone. Out in the front lobby, Doug started to exit the building. "Excuse me, but you need to sit down, I am calling your parents right now to come pick you up." Doug flipped her off and sat in a chair. He was going to get even with Homer if it was the last thing he did. Darla picked up the phone and dialed out, Doug tried to listen, but could not hear anything. He sat there stewing for some time, thinking about how he could get even with Homer. He would like to take out the principle too, but he did not know how. He had been looking forward to this prom all year and asked out the sexiest girl in school, Sheila. If only he could just kill that scrawny little runt for doing this to him. Then he got a brilliant idea. He would get Homer suspended too. That jerk was looking forward to going to the prom, he thought. He would fix it where he would not be able to go either. He thought about a moment longer, then it hit him. He knew where Homer's locker was, and he could plant some drugs there, he still had some at home, and this would be a great way to get even with him. He smiled to himself; this was a perfect plan. He thought about what he had in his stash. He still had some weed, and that would get Homer expelled for sure. The smile disappeared from his face when he looked up and saw his dad pull up in the parking lot. The shit was going to hit the fan, he thought. His dad was a big man and he noticed that he looked angry as he got out of his car and approached the office doors. When he came in, Doug crouched down in the chair. "Well," his dad said, "Get your ass up out of that chair, you can explain to me what an idiot you have been on the way home." As Doug stood up, Darla smiled from behind the desk. In the back of her mind, she always thought that Doug was a little shithead and she hoped his dad was going to beat his ass. She did not like bullies, she had bullied herself as a little girl when she was in school. His dad caught a glimpse of her smiling and shot a dirty look her way. She cleared her throat and looked back down at her desk. With that, the two of them exited the office. Darla watched then as they got into his car and drove off. She knew he was being scolded, and she thought to herself, that was not enough. He should have been bullwhipped for what he had done to that poor boy.

2

DOUG SAT IN HIS ROOM, his father had given him a good tongue lashing and of all things, grounded him. He was totally pissed; Homer was going to pay for this. He riffled around through his room to find his stash. He opened a drawer in his dresser and there it was, a little baggie full of Marijuana, he smiled at his find. Now he just needed to get a hold of John somehow and get him to plant this in Homer's locker. He looked at his watch, one thirty, he would be in fifth period right now, he thought. He could get him to cut sixth period and come over to give him the stash, but how was he going to get him a message, he thought. He looked over at his phone, his parents had one installed in his room over last summer, he had taken a job at Steve's Market, the one by the bus stop, to help pay for it. He enjoyed having his own phone. His room was large, he had a double bed and two dressers. On one dresser sat a small TV with a VCR and his video game hooked up to it, something he had bought himself. On the other dresser sat his phone. He walked over to it and picked up the receiver, he had to think for a moment, what was he going to say, and would Darla know it was him. He practiced his voice a few different times. "Yes, excuse me, but I need a message given to John Templan please, this is his father and I need to meet him in the parking lot after fifth period." This did not sound right; he would get caught for sure. He cleared his throat and tried it a little deeper. "Hello, this is John Templan's father, and I need him to come to the parking lot before sixth period to give him his homework." He smiled, he thought this sounded better, but it had to sound really good to fool Darla. This was not going to work, he thought. Even if he could fool Darla, how was going to get to the parking lot of the high school, then he looked at his watch again, in fifteen minutes? He thought about it for another minute, then he decided he would just leave, there was no possible way his dad would catch him. He turned on the tv and then the video game system. He plugged in a cartridge into the system and pushed start. The video game came to life, and he turned up the volume on the tv just enough so it could be heard from outside of his room. He opened the window and slowly crept out. His home was only one story and his bedroom window opened into the back yard. He removed the screen years ago when he used to sneak out to get high with his girlfriend. He stood in the yard and looked around to make sure the coast was clear, then he took off for the back gate. He had a bicycle on the other side of the gate, and he thought that he could make it to the high school within the next fifteen minutes. He climbed onto his bike and took off. He peddled as fast as he could so he could make it to the high school and then get back home before his dad would catch him.

Sotterville High School was rather large with over two thousand students. It had stood here for almost one hundred years, established in 1891, it had grown from one building to fifteen buildings, two gyms, a swimming pool, and an agricultural department that had three green houses. In more recent years they received enough funding to add a wood shop and a metal shop for anyone who wanted to learn a trade. Plans had been developed to add another building that would house classes for electrical shops. There were even talks about adding a house wiring class as well once the new building was up and running. Overall, this high school was large enough that it took up almost three city blocks. The front of the school had two separate parking lots, one between the main office and the library, and the second one in front of the science building. In the back by the cafeteria was another large parking lot that sat between the cafeteria and boys' gym. John was in his fifth period class, which was a cooking class. It sat two buildings behind the library. He took a lot of flak for taking a cooking class, but it was one that he really enjoyed, and he just did not care what anyone thought. The class itself was large, and had ten kitchens set up, five on each side of the room. Each kitchen had its own stove with an oven, a sink, a refrigerator, and counter space with cabinets above and below. In the center of each kitchen was a round table that could sit up to four people. The door to the classroom was on the right side. There was no back door or any windows on the side with the doors. There was a row of windows on the opposite side of the room that ran the whole length of the classroom. The teacher's station was at the front of the classroom, and in the back of the classroom was a washer and dryer to clean the kitchen towels that were used during class. John sat at kitchen number six that was on the left side of the room by the windows, opposite the side with the door. His teacher, Mrs. Hollingsworth, was at the front and was in the middle of tasting a piece of cake. This was the recipe of the day, and John was proud of what he had created. He was earning an A in the class and was really proud of that. He thought about being a chef when he got older and had considered going to culinary art school. The main reason that he had taken classes with this teacher all four years of high school was that deep down inside, he had a huge crush on her. He was always volunteering during lunch period to come in and do odds and ends for her. He would clean the kitchens, wash dishes, and help her file recipes. He was listening to the teacher critique this cake when he heard a tapping on the window. He turned and looked and saw Doug standing there. He motioned for John to meet him in the parking lot outside by the cafeteria when class was over. John shook his head, then turned back to listen to Mrs. Hollingsworth again. She stood about five feet five inches with bright red hair. John thought she was the perfect woman, once he could love every day and never get tired of. He looked at her with dreamy eyes hanging on every word she said. "This cake is moist, it has all the ingredients, however; the frosting is a little grainy which means that you did not cook the sugar long enough before you added the cocoa. Very good, but table number four, I expect better from you." At that, the bell rang. Everyone put their stuff back into their backpacks and everyone stood to leave. "Don't forget, the rest of this week we will be making cupcakes for the prom.

See you all tomorrow." John waved to her as he walked out. He headed for the back parking lot. He would have to hurry, his next class was in the ag building on the other side of the campus, and he only had six minutes in between bells. He saw Doug standing next to the blue pickup, he had laid his bike on the ground, and was leaning against the truck. "What's up? I heard you got suspended." Doug shoved him. "Yeah, you should have too, you jerk." John liked him, but he didn't like being shoved around by him, and he especially did not like being called a jerk. "Listen, I want to get that creep, so here is something I need you to stick in his locker." He handed the little bag to John, who took it and put it in his pocket. "What is it?" Doug looked around to make sure there was no one close by. "It is my last three ounces of weed. This is enough to get that moron expelled for the rest of the year." John's eyes lit up, "I see, then he won't be able to go to the prom either." Doug shook his head yes at this. "I really would like to wring his neck until the light goes out of his eyes, but this will be just as good." "Right, get him where it hurts. But listen, how are you going to make him get caught?" Doug had not thought about this part, he would have to have someone inform the principal, or he could call the police and give an anonymous tip. "You know, I think I will call the front office and let them know that I saw it, or?" he looked at John, "you can call and give them the tip, maybe even say that he sold you some." John smiled, that would be the best way he thought. "I can do that, but I got to get to it." he looked at his watch, "I only have three minutes before the next bell." Doug patted John on his head, "You go then, thanks for helping me out on this one, that creep is going to have a great surprise." He turned and got on his bike then took off. John knew where Homer's locker was, it was over in the building where the art classes were, which was on the way to the ag department. He walked as quick as he could, and once he got back into the hallways, he did his best to avoid everyone. He turned down the hallway that led to the lockers down by the art rooms. There were five classes in all in this building. The building was large itself and had classrooms on each side. There were lockers in between each class, with four art rooms, and the choir class at the end of the building. He stood back and made sure that there was no one watching. Homer's locker was number 518 in between two of the art classes. Once he saw that there was no one looking, he pulled the bag from his pocket and walked over to the lockers. The lockers were two feet tall each, stacked two at a time, in rows of eight, with sixteen in total for each bay. There were two sets of vents in each locker that were at least three inches in length and an inch and half wide. He looked around again and when he felt no one was watching, he stuffed the bag in the bottom vent, then pushed it till it went all the way inside. He looked around again, then he took off.

John decided that he would be late for class and went across the street to the Dairy Freez to use the pay phone. He fished a quarter from his pocket, picked up the receiver, dropped in the coin, and dialed the school's number. The Dairy Freeze was a small local burger joint that had been here for almost fifty years. It did a great business as the high schoolers ate her during the school year for lunch, rather than eating in the cafeteria on the campus. There were other burger joints on the opposite side of the street in front of the high school, but this one sat on the right side, close to the auditorium and the ag department. The phone rang and Darla answered. "Sotterville High School, you have reached the front office, how can I help you?" John thought about it and thought he should mask his voice. He put his hand over the receiver and then talked through it. "I just want to let you know that I bought an ounce of weed from one of you students, I met him at locker 518. He still has about three ounces. You should check it out." Then he hung up. He smiled, looked at his watch, then took off for his class.

In the office, Darla hung up the phone. She had taken calls like this before, but it was better to be safe than sorry. She picked up her phone and pressed the button marked Payne. "Yes," he said. "I have some information for you that you might want to know, not sure how

true it is, but something like this, I think you should check it out."
"What is going on?" he asked. "I just got a phone call from someone
who said they just bought an ounce of drugs from one of our students."
Mr. Payne thought about it for a moment, then he answered her. "Yes,
you are right, we don't want any more of that kind of trouble, let me
get my bolt cutters and I will meet you in just a moment." She hung
up the phone and stood up, she had written down the locker number
on a small note pad, she tore it off and picked it up. Mr. Payne walked
out from the inner office and met her at her desk. "Did they give you
a name or a locker number?" She held up the notepad and gave it
to him. He read it and then handed it back to her. "Okay, let's go."
They left the office and headed for locker number 518. When they
arrived at the location of the locker, Mr. Payne took the bolt cutters
and with one snap, cut the lock. Darla took the bolt cutters from him
and then handed him a pair of rubber gloves. He looked over the locker
as he put the gloves on, inspecting what he could see. Once he had
the gloves on, he began rifling through the books and papers that had
been stuffed inside. Then he stumbled across the little baggie John
had stuffed inside. He held it up to inspect it. He let out a deep sigh,
"Looks like about two or three ounces here. Who is assigned to this
locker?" Darla thought about it for a moment. She wished she would
have grabbed her clipboard with the printout of locker assignments. "I
am not sure; I will have to look it up when we get back to the office."
He shook his head, stuffed the bag in his shirt pocket, and they headed
back to the office.

Mr. Payne sat behind his desk going through some paperwork he
needed to finish when his phone rang. "Yes." he said when he picked
up the receiver. "That locker belongs to Homer Fenstra." Mr. Payne
suddenly had an ill look on his face. He had always known Homer to
be one of his better students. He wondered what had made him turn
to drugs like this. "Okay Darla, look at his schedule and find out what
class he is in right now, then send for him." "Sure, thing sir." she said

and quickly hung up. He debated calling the police, after all, they had some trouble with some drugs a few months ago. It even involved the death of a student who had taken his own life. He had taken something that sent him off on a really bad trip. He had climbed to the top of the school's auditorium and then leaped off. He realized that it was something he may have been able to prevent, had he listened to one of the students who had complained about the drug use in the school. But at the time, he could not believe that his school could have a problem like this. So now, if they had any reports, no matter where it came from, they checked it out. He picked up the phone and began to dial the police station but had a change of heart. He would just give Homer a suspension and let him know that this kind of behavior would not be tolerated at his school. There was a knock on the door as he put the receiver back onto the phone. "Come in." The door opened and Homer walked in. "Please son, take a seat." Homer sheepishly walked over to one of the two chairs that sat in front of the desk. "Do you know why I called you here, Homer?" he asked, his voice as calm as he could get it. Homer shook his head no. Mr. Payne picked up the bag of Marijuana from his desk and held it up so Homer could see it. "Do you know what this is?" he asked, again, his voice as cool as he could make it. Again, Homer shook his head no. "Well son," he went on, "This is Marijuana and I found it in your locker." Homer suddenly got very defensive, "Mr. Payne, that is not mine, I don't know where that came from, you got to believe me." Homer stood up. Mr. Payne put up his hand, "Please, calm down. It does not matter if it is yours or not, the fact is we got a phone call that someone bought some of this from you, and when we searched your locker, we found this. Now normally I would call the police, but since this is the first time you have been found with this, and since you are a good student with no prior records, I am not going to call the police, however; what I am going to do is give you a three day suspension, which means you will not be able to go to the prom, if you were planning on it." Homer sat down; he began to sob. "I have never been in trouble before." he said, as he tried to hold back his tears. "I understand that son, that is why I am being so lenient with you this time. But I have to tell you, if this happens again, I will call the police and you will have to face them, do you understand that?" Homer shook his head. He wiped the tears from his cheeks, he felt embarrassed, he did not like to cry in front of people. "So, I won't be able to go to the prom?" Homer asked. Mr. Payne took a napkin out of his desk drawer and handed it to him, "That's right son, you will not be able to go." Homer took the napkin and blew his nose, then he stood up. He made an angry face at Mr. Payne, then he turned and ran from the office. Payne picked up his phone and dialed Darla, "Listen, Homer just ran out, catch him so we can call his parents." But it was too late, Homer had already dashed from the office and Darla could not catch him.

As he ran through the main door, he threw the napkin he was holding to the ground. He stopped at the front of the school and looked around, looking for a place to go. He took off down the street and headed towards the Dairy Freeze. A few seconds later, Darla and Mr. Payne came bursting through the office doors, "You look over there" Payne pointed to the left side of the school by the library, "I will look across the street, if we don't find him, I will call his parents, I am sure he ran home." With that, Darla headed towards the library and Payne headed for the street. When he reached the edge of the sidewalk, he looked to his left and his right of the street to see if he could see Homer but did not see anything. He began to walk up and down the sidewalk, looking in every direction. He was not going to chase anyone down but wanted to give it his best shot. He did not actually cross the street itself, just looked everywhere. There were several fast-food restaurants and a few stores across the street from the high school, several shrubs and trees. In between the traffic, he looked to see if anyone was behind the trees or the shrubs while also peering at the restaurants. When he did not see him, he turned to walk away. One of the businesses was a video game arcade, this was also where there were several shrubs as well. From behind the shrubs, there were a pair of eyes watching Mr. Payne as he was looking up and down the street. They watched as he gave up and he headed back towards the office. "Did you see anything?" Darla shook her head. "Okay, well let's write up the report and call out to his parents." She shook her head again, and they both walked inside the office.

3

It was about seven thirty Monday night, and Doug was sitting in his room playing his video game. He always thought that others were jealous because he owned a video game system. He did not care though, it just meant that he did not have to spend his money at the video game arcade that was across the street from the high school. He thought back, if he had saved all those quarters, he spent in that palace he could have bought two systems. Of course, they had bigger and better games, plus some of the ones that he fondly remembered when he was younger and his family would go out for pizza. The pizza place had a game room in the back that always had five or six arcade games. He had spent a small fortune in quarters there too. He had become upset that he had not heard from John to see if his plan had worked or not. If it did not work, not only was he going to just beat the crap out of Homer, but he was going to beat the crap out of John too for lousing it up. His phone rang and he paused his game to answer it. "Hello." There was nothing. "Hello!" he said again. He listened intently and could hear someone breathing on the other end of the line. "Listen shithead, if you don't say anything, I am going to hang up on you." He was getting irritated, and it carried over in his voice. Still there was nothing but the sound of breathing on the other end. "Okay asshole, you don't want to talk, that is fine with me, just don't call this number again." With that he hung up the phone. He huffed as he picked up his controller and un-paused his game to start again. The phone rang again, and he dropped the controller and picked up the receiver, "Who the hell is, and why do you keep calling me?" he answered. "Calm down assface, it's me John. So, I got the stuff planted on him, and guess what?" "I don't want to play, so just tell me." "So, I heard that they suspended Homer, then he took off running, no one knows where he is. He was crying so bad." Doug started laughing at this, "Right on!" he said, "Hope he ran home to his mommy! What a loser." "Well, hey, I just thought I would share the good news with you man, besides, now that he is suspended, he can't go to the prom either." "Hey John, shut your face. Besides, I am going to the prom, you think that asshole principle can keep me from going?" "Well, how are you going to get in?" "You are going to help me get in you putz, you will sneak me into the cafeteria through the back door." "And what if the principal catches me?" Doug thought about that for a moment, he could care less if John got into trouble, that would be his own fault. "Nothing, you won't do anything." John didn't like this answer, he didn't understand why he hung out with this asshole anyway. "Fine, but let me tell you something, if I get caught, you will get caught too." John did not answer him and was silent. "Look, meet in the morning in front of the arcade, I will give you something for your trouble." "Like what?" John asked. Doug thought about it for a moment, then answered him. "I know you like a little smack once in a while, I will bring you some in the morning, just meet me there before first period and I will bring you some." "Listen Doug, I don't do that anymore. You want to bring me something, bring me Sheila." This made Doug even more upset, how dare John talk about his girlfriend like this. "I am not bringing you my girlfriend. She wouldn't touch you with a ten-foot pole you asswipe, just meet me at eight, I will take care of you." "I don't think I can get you into the prom Doug. It doesn't matter what you bring me." Doug didn't like this answer and hung up on him. Screw him, he thought. He would just get himself into the prom some other way. Besides, he wasn't going to let his girlfriend be there without him. "Oh shit!" he said out loud. He looked at his watch, he was supposed to call Sheila a half an hour ago, she was going to be pissed, he thought. He picked up the phone and dialed her number. As the phone rang, he looked at his watch again. It rang about ten times, and when there was no answer, he slammed the phone back into the cradle. He looked around the room, not sure what he was looking for. Then he looked at his window, he could sneak out again and ride his bike over to Sheila's house. It would take about fifteen minutes as she lived over on the east side of town. He looked down at his watch again, if he left right now, he would be at her house by eight. He went over to his bedroom door and opened it slightly. Peering out, he checked to see if anyone was around. He did not see anyone; his parents were most likely in their room doing heaven knows what. He closed the door softly. This time, he locked his bedroom door, during the day, no one bothered him, but sometimes at night, his mother would check in on him. He would always tell her that he was old enough to take care of himself, but she insisted that was what a good mother would do. He walked over to his dresser and clicked on the TV. Looking around his room, he spied an old video tape with one of his favorite movies on it. He grabbed and threw it into the VCR. The screen lit up with the whole FBI warning message, then he turned the volume up just a little. This would make his parents believe he was in here watching TV. The movie lasted about two hours and he felt that this would give him plenty of time to sneak out, ride over to Sheila's, hang out for a while, then get back before the movie was over. He smiled, this was perfect, he thought. He sashayed over to his window and opened it up. He was met with a blast of warm air. He frowned; he hated this valley weather. Here it was a quarter to eight, and it was still ninety degrees outside. He shook his head as he climbed through the window. After he crawled through, he shut it about mid-way, this would make it easy for him to get back inside. He slowly checked out the yard, something he should have done before he exited his room, he thought, just to make sure no one was outside. It was still daylight out, and he would have at least till almost ten before it would start to get dark. He looked over by the back gate to the alley and realized his bike was not there. He frowned, where was it? He looked over the entire backyard, then he realized that his dad must have put it in the shed. He wondered if his dad had realized that he snuck out earlier. He looked back down at his watch, he did not have time to sit and think about it, Sheila was way more important, he could talk with his dad later about it.

He walked over to the shed and went to take the lock off, but he noticed that it was already unlocked, and that the lock was hanging on the hook. That was strange, he thought. He had a key and was getting ready to take it out of his pocket. His dad never left the shed unlocked. He looked around the yard again just to double check to make sure that there was no one watching him. He looked at all the windows of the house to see if maybe his dad was trying to catch him leave again. He did not see anything. He opened the door slowly, peered inside to see if anyone was there, but the light was off, so he walked in. There was only one window in the shed and his dad had it covered with tin foil over the winter and had not taken it off yet. He said it helped to keep the shed warmer and prevented the heat from his small wood stove from escaping. Doug just thought that maybe his dad was smoking dope and didn't want anyone to see. It was dark in the shed with no light, except for the sunlight that was coming through the open door. He fumbled around the light switch, and when he clicked it on, there was nothing. "Shit." he said. He tried to get his eyes adjusted to the darkness so he could see where his bike was. He looked around the shed, there were mostly gardening tools, the lawn mower, and a few of his dad's car parts laying on a table. His dad had bought an old 1957 Chevy a few years ago and was trying to restore it, without much luck. It seemed that every time that he had made progress on it, he would run into another problem. First it was the transmission, then it was the starter. He would pull off parts that were rusty and could not find a replacement for them, so he was trying to fix those parts. Doug had always thought it was a waste of time. He continued to look for his bike and that is when he spotted it. It was leaning up against the wall next to a tarp that his dad had opened. He had owned several tarps in the past and he always had them completely open and unfolded and hanging from the rafters. He had always thought it was creepy that his dad did this, but he said he helped to keep it dry and keep the spiders out of it. As he walked over to the bike, he thought he saw the tarp move. That was funny he thought, he could not feel any wind and wondered what could make the tarp move like that. He shrugged it off and started to reach out for the handlebars of the bike. Suddenly, a gloved hand was clasped over his mouth, and he could not make any noise.

4

Detective Miller sat behind his desk at the police station looking over some old files when his phone rang. He picked up the receiver, "Give it to me." he said, as perky as he could on a Monday night at ten PM. "Got a few minutes you can spare Miller?" came the voice from the other end of the phone. He looked down at his desk, looked over at the clock on the wall, then let out a deep sigh, "Sure, what you got?" "We had a report of a missing teenager, my partner and I are getting ready to head over but thought you might want to come along." He thought for a moment, "Why do you want me to come along?" "Well, you are kind of the expert on this sort of stuff, you know, a kind of detective, thought this would be right up your alley." "All right, let me get my hat and I will be right with you." He stood up from his desk and grabbed his hat off of the hat rack that stood next to his office door. He walked through the squad room thinking how a cup of coffee sounded good right about now. He stepped out into the parking lot and saw that there were two police officers leaning up against his car. "What, you want to take my car?" He was a plain clothes detective who drove a 1980 Chrysler, unmarked as well. The two officers were Bradock and Duncan. "Well, we could go in the squad car, but we thought it was a little too inconspicuous." Duncan said, about to laugh out loud. "Inconspicuous my ass, now where are we heading?" Bradock pulled the report from his pocket and read it to Miller. "So, the parents of one Doug Burton, they went into his room about nine thirty this evening and he was nowhere to be found. Said they called a few of his friends, girlfriend, that sort of thing, no one else has seen him." "Do you know if they touched anything?" Miller asked as he opened the driver side door. "Nope, don't know anything, won't know till we get there." As Miller got behind the wheel and started the car, he looked over at Duncan who was getting into the front seat, "Well, you haven't told me where there is?" Bradock smiled, "Oh yeah, Springville drive, 1462." He shut the door and Miller took off leaving Duncan behind.

He flipped off the car as it drove out of the parking lot then headed back inside.

When they approached the house, they could see the mother sitting on the front step. Miller noticed that it looked like she had been crying. "Let me do the talking." Miller said. Bradock was fine with letting him do the talking, he didn't like doing the talking anyway. She stood up as they exited the car and met them as they ascended the steps to the front porch. "Hello, I am detective Don Miller." He reached out his hand and she did the same. "This is officer Bradock who will be assisting me during this investigation. What can you tell me?" She cleared her throat and wiped the tears from her face, then looked up at him. Miller stood over six feet five inches, he was a rather large man, she thought. He had broad shoulders and was dressed in a suit and tie and wore a hat that reminded her of old detective movies, the kind you saw on Sunday afternoon television. He took a notebook and pencil from his coat pocket and began to take some notes as she spoke. "Well, he was suspended from school today, so of course his father grounded him. He had dinner with us around six, then went back to his room. Around nine-thirty I went in to say goodnight, but his door was locked. I knocked and when there was no answer, I got a key and let myself in. His window was halfway open, and he was nowhere to be found. I called his best friend's house and his girlfriend's house, neither of them has seen him since this morning at school." Miller wrote all this down, then asked, "Tell me more about your son Mrs. Burton." "Well, he is 18, he was the captain of the football team. He is about five feet ten inches, blond hair, blue eyes, and a small scar on his right arm, just above his wrist. He got that when he was fourteen from playing football. He was tackled and fell onto a piece of glass that had somehow got onto the field." Miller looked at her with symptomatic eyes and smiled slightly. "What was he wearing the last time you saw him?" She looked down, then looked back at him, "His football jersey, number 21, and a pair of jeans." Miller wrote this down, then put the pad back in his office along with the pen, then looked around the front of the house, and then back to her. "Do you mind if we take a look around?" The sun was setting and it was beginning to get dark and Miller took a flashlight out of his coat and Bradock did the same. "Sure," she sniffed and wiped her nose, "I will show you to his room." She turned and headed for the front door with Miller and Bradock following. She walked them through the front door, Miller took in the house as he walked through. The front door opened up into the living room, off to the right was the dining room and the kitchen. She led them to the hallway just behind the living room. Miller looked at the pictures that hung on the hall and when he saw one of Doug he stopped. "Is this your son?" She turned and looked, "Yes." She said, "His room is the last one on the right." She led them to the room, opened the door, and the two police walked in.

Miller took in the whole room. The TV was still on, there was no picture, and it was just snow on the screen. The VCR had stopped, rewound the tape, and it had ejected and turned off. He looked over the rest of the room, the bed, the closet, then the window. He turned to Bradrock, "I want you to dust for prints around that window frame, and also the TV and VCR. I want to know if he was kidnapped, if they used the TV and VCR to hide the fact he was gone." He turned back to Mrs. Burton, "Has Doug ever ran away from home before?" She shook her head no. "Has there been any strange phone calls, people hanging up?" She thought for a moment, then shook her head no again. Then her eyes lit up like she remembered something important. "Doug has his own phone and his own phone number, but he has never said anything about prank calls." She pointed to the phone on the dresser. Miller looked over it and then turned back to Bradock. "I want you to get a hold of the phone company and pull the records for that phone." Bradcock shook his head, then Miller looked back over to Doug's mother. "Where does that window lead?" "It goes out to the backyard." Miller looked over at Bradock, "Take care of this room, I am going to check out the backyard." She led him back down the hallway to the kitchen where the back door was. She flipped on the light and he turned on his flashlight. When they walked outside, Miller looked around the yard. He noticed the gate that led to the alley and the shed. "Do you keep your back gate and your shed locked at all times?" "No, well we keep the shed locked at all times, only my husband and Doug have keys. And we have never locked the back gate." Miller shone his light over the back gate, it was closed, then he moved the light over to the shed, the door was open wide. "I thought you said the shed was always locked?" She looked and saw that it was open. "We do." She started to walk over to the shed, Miller held his hand out to stop her. "You stay here, let me go and check this out." He lifted his light and walked over to the shed. When he reached the door, he shone his light inside before he walked in. He looked around for the light switch, when he found it, he flipped the switch, and the light did not come on.

He left the switch alone and used his flashlight to look around. He looked over and saw Doug's bike leaning against the wall next to a tarp that was hanging from the rafters. As he walked towards the bike, he noticed that tarp moved slightly. He stopped just short of the tarp and shone his light on it. He approached it slowly, shining his light from side to side, watching both his left and right sides. When he reached the tarp, he reached out slowly and pulled it back, shining his light in every direction. There was nothing there. He released the tarp from his grip, and he caught something on the floor out of the corner of his eye. He shone his light on the floor and saw something that looked like a small drop of blood. He got down on one knee to take a closer look at the spot on the floor when he felt a hand fall on his shoulder. He shone his flashlight behind him and turned quickly to look. It was just Bradock. "Haven't I ever told you not to sneak up on people like that?" Bradock smiled, then looked down at the floor. "Yes, you have, but I couldn't help myself. What you have here?" Miller stood up. "We need to get a forensics team down here; this looks like a drop of blood. I want you to seal off this shed, don't let anyone in here, and we are going to treat this as murder until we have some answers." Bradock looked at him squarely, "Murder? I just thought maybe this kid ran off. I picked up two sets of prints in the bedroom, five will get you ten, It is Doug's and his mother's prints. But I will take them over to the lab and get the forensics team down here to go over this shed, but I can tell you right now, it will be in the morning." Miller shook his head, "Listen Bradock, if this was anything else I would say no big deal. But if this is murder, don't you think we ought to start on it now?" Bradock took a deep breath. "Yes." They started to leave the shed when Miller looked over and saw Doug's mother. "You stay here, wait for the team, I will talk to the mother." Bradock shook his head in agreement and then reached for his walkie talky. Miller walked over to the mom, who was doing her best to not cry. "Not to worry Mrs. Burton, we are going to look into everything. In the meantime, I think you and your husband maybe take in a motel tonight, on us." She could not hold it in any longer and started to cry. Miller put his hand on her shoulder, and she placed her head on his. He never liked this part, but he did his best. "Please, you and your husband take the night off, we need to go over a few things and we may be here a while." She lifted her head and her eyes met his, "Is he dead?" He did not want to startle her or make things worse, so he chose his words really carefully. "At this point I am going to say no, but we want to go over everything, meet with his girlfriend, and go down to the high school in the morning and find out why he was suspended. We are going to do everything we can to find your son." She sniffled, wiped her eyes, then turned and went into the house. Miller looked around the yard again, then looked over the house. Bradock walked up to Miller as he was looking around. "So, what do you think?" Miller looked over at him. "Right now, no clues, no suspects, no nothing, I got nothing. A missing teenager, a blood spot on the floor of a shed that was supposed to be locked, I have absolutely nothing." He looked over the yard again, checking to see if there was anything he missed. Not seeing anything, he left Bradock in charge, looked over the house one more time, then left.

5

There was a blaring, beeping sound that erupted from the alarm clock that sat on the table next to Mr. Payne's bed. He slowly opened his eyes and looked at his clock, it was six thirty in the morning and he had a busy day ahead of him. Reaching over, he tapped the clock once to shut off the annoying sound that woke him from his dream. He had been the principal at the high school for almost ten years, and it was not a bad job, but he had his troubled students that he just could not stand. There had been some students that he wished he could have hit with a two by four upside their heads, but he knew that would solve their problems. He looked over on the other side of the bed, his wife was already up. He stood from his bed, got dressed and headed out of the bedroom to the kitchen. His wife was making some toast, when she saw him, she poured him a glass of orange juice. "It's about time you got up, sleepy head." He looked at her and gave her a smirk, picked up the orange juice, and gulped it down. "How did I miss the alarm?" he asked. She looked at him and smiled. "You were sleeping pretty heavy, and you came in so late last night, so I shut it off before it went off, thought I would give you some extra time." He put his hand on her ass and gave it a pat. "Thank you, I really needed it. Hope I didn't wake you when I got in?" "I was not really asleep, so you are all good. But listen to this. I was listening to the news this morning, that kid you said you suspended yesterday, guess he came up missing last night." Harold looked at her in a strange way. "Which one?" "Remember, you called me from the office yesterday and you told me that you had to suspend that idiot that had been torturing other students, you said his name was Doug right." Harold shook his head, "How do you know they meant him?" "Well, the reporter said that after he went missing last night, the police were investigating it, and the parents, the Burtons, they were on the news too, asking people to help look for him." "Well, maybe he ran away from home, some eighteen-year-olds have been known to do that." He took his piece of toast and began to eat it. "Well, I hope they find him." Harold didn't say anything, his mouth was full, and he just shook his head in agreement. "I have to go in a little early this morning, I just hate this time of the school year." She looked at him funny, "I always thought you liked it when the year was over?" "Well, technically I do, but I also hate it. It is a pain ending the year out, and then there is always getting ready for the prom, that is a total pain too." He picked up his briefcase from the counter, kissed his wife, and then headed for the door. She watched him as he left.

On his drive to work, Harold had the radio on to try and listen to the news, but he could not find anything about Doug. He smirked to himself. When he reached the school parking lot, he was surprised to see two police cars and a news truck. He parked in his normal spot and looked over; he could see Darla talking to plainclothes officer. He shut off his car and grabbed his briefcase, got out, then walked over to them. "What is going on here?" he asked. The officer reached out his hand to shake his. "Hello, I am detective Miller, your secretary called the police this morning. When she got here, she found this message." He pointed to the ground. Harold looked down, written in what looked like red paint on the sidewalk was a message. It read:

"Cancel the prom while you have time, one is gone, and others are in line."

Harold read the message, then looked at Miller. "What does that mean, one is gone, and others are in line?" Miller looked at him, "I cannot share anything with you at this time, but it seems like you may want to consider canceling the prom." Harold looked at him with a dead serious face. "As much as I would like to shut the dance down, I have an obligation to the students of this high school, and they would be really upset if I did that, so here is what will happen. You find the person who wrote this graffiti on the sidewalk and I want them charged with vandalism. Sound like a plan to you?" Miller looked at him then looked at Darla, "Well I can't force you to shut it down, at least not yet, but if there is anything else, I could get a court order." Harold shook his head; it would be a cold day in hell before the court would actually shut down a high school dance. He watched as a police photographer took pictures of the sidewalk from all angles. Then another man came over and bent down, took something out of his pants pocket. He thought it looked like a razor. The man scraped some of the paint off of the sidewalk and put it into a test tube. He turned back towards Miller, "Listen, I tell you what, I will keep an eye on everything on my end, you on your end. If there is anything that shouts out like a real concern, I will take canceling the prom into serious consideration. After all, I don't want any of the students getting hurt either, you know." "That is good to hear Mr. Payne." Miller turned to Darla, "Was this the only message?" She shook her head yes. The team they had brought was finishing up, Miller put his pen and pad back into his coat pocket, "Looks like we got everything we need from you. We will have the paint analyzed, that could lead us to who might have done this. In the meantime," he looked squarely at Harold, "if there is anything else, you will let us know, and we will have the prom shut down." Harold shook his yes, "I also need to talk to you about one of your students, if you have a moment?" Miller said, looking over at Darla. "Sure, let's go in my office." Harold turned to Darla, "Why didn't you call me first?" "I did, but your wife said you were sleeping, so I called the cops." He gave her a dirty look, "We will talk about this later, when they are all finished, and have someone clean this shit up."

Miller followed Harold into the main building, as they walked through the office, Miller took note of everything. As they stepped into Harold's office, he shut the door behind him. "I need some information about Doug Burton, I understand he was suspended yesterday, is this correct?' Harold sat down behind his desk while Miller remained standing. "Yes, he had some trouble on the bus ride to school yesterday?" "What kind of trouble?" Miller asked. "Well, he assaulted another student, there was a fight and he ended up punching the other student." Miller began to take more interest in this and sat down. "Was this the first time he had this kind of behavior?" Harold shook his head, "No, as a matter of fact, it was the third time he had done something like this, that is why I suspended him." Miller took out his notepad and pencil and began writing, "And who was the other student?" "The other student was Homer Fenstra." Miller looked up sharply, "And where is Homer now?" Harold shook his head, "That I am unsure of, you see, we found a substantial amount of marijuana in his locker and he was also suspended. We tried to reach his parents, but there was no answer, and Homer ran off." Miller wrote this down, "And, have you tried to call his parents since?" Harold thought about this for a moment, then he answered, "No, we just thought he went home. We did try to go after him, but we were unsuccessful." Miller stood to his feet, "I will need the boys address and phone number if you please." Harold stood up, "You can get that from Darla out front, she has all of his information." Miller turned to go, "I would advise you to think twice about shutting down the prom, I will keep in touch with you."

Miller approached Bradock, who was leaning against his car. "What do you think about this?" Miller thought for a moment, then looked around to see if anyone else was paying attention. "The message said, one is gone. You don't suppose it was talking about that Burton kid do you?' Miller still had not answered yet, he looked around again, then leaned in close to Bradock. "Listen, I do not know if the two are connected, but I don't want the parents to find out about this. Also, there is another boy missing, his name is Homer Fenstra, he and Doug got into an altercation on the bus yesterday, both boys had been suspended. I have his address, it is 1635 Springville drive, I want you to keep everything under wraps, and then check out that address. I will talk to you later" Bradock looked over at the news van. "Well, we are a little late on that one. I will do what I can, and then check out that address." He sighed heavily, "Right. I hate reporters." Miller looked over at the news van in disgust, "They always screw up our investigations. Regardless, do your best to do some damage control on this just in case they ask. As for it being connected, like I said, I don't know yet. But one thing is for sure, let's hope this person is not serious." Bradock shook his head, "I am good at damage control." Miller smiled at him. Another officer walked up and tapped Miller on the shoulder. "Excuse me sir, I have all I can get from here, I am going to get this back to the lab, is there anything else you need from me before I go?" Miller thought about this for a moment. "No, I suppose we should get everyone out of here before the students decide to show up, we don't need a bigger circus than we already have." He agreed, then turned and left. "So you are good at damage control, huh? Well, get that reporter out of here, put a lid on this, and go check on the Burton's." Bradock smiled and walked away. Miller stood there puzzling for a moment. He wanted to know who wrote the message, and if it really did have something to do with that missing boy. He looked over at the office and thought about going into there and talking to the principal some more, then he stopped himself. There was no solid concrete evidence to show that the two incidents were related. He climbed into his car, started it up and headed back to the squad room.

Harold and Darla sat in his office. He was behind his desk and she sat on the opposite side of him. He opened his bottom desk drawer, which was also a file cabinet, and pulled out a piece of paper. "So I will need you to fill out this incident report. I want every detail about this in there. When you got here, when you found it, and when you called the police." She stood up and walked around to where he was sitting. He looked up at her, she was younger than he was, about five years. She had jet back hair that fell about shoulder length, and when she leaned over him to look at the paper, it brushed up against his face. He looked at her and noticed that the top three buttons of her blouse were open and her breasts were exposed. She glanced over at him, feeling his eyes on her. He noticed her looking and quickly turned his head. He cleared his throat, "Fill this out and get it back to me as soon as you can, thank you Darla." She turned so she could face him, then she pushed back his chair away from the desk, then sat in his lap. As her lips met his, he could feel his pulse rise. He could not believe this, she had never done this before. Midway through their passionate kiss, his phone rang. He gently pushed her away and reached for the phone. She stood up and buttoned back up her blouse. "Mr. Payne, how can I help you?" There was silence on the other end. "Hello." he said again. There was still no answer, and he quickly hung up the phone. When he did, there was a knock on the door. Darla picked up the incident report and headed for the door. "See you later sir." She said as she opened the door. The reporter was standing at the door. He was an older man, his salt and peppered hair was well trimmed, and he stood about six feet tall. "Am I interrupting anything?" he asked, as he walked in. "Uh, no." "Great." He walked in and Darla walked out. He sat in the chair opposite Mr. Payne, then he retrieved his notebook from his shirt pocket along with a pencil. "What can I do for you?" Harold said, annoyed that he just barged in. "Well, the police kindly asked me to leave, but I thought I should at least ask you a couple of questions before I go." "Well I don't know if I will be much help, but go ahead." He put the pencil to the pad and then began grilling Harold. "So, I heard from an inside source that you suspended two students yesterday, is that correct?" Who told this moron about that, he thought? "Well, I really can't talk about that." The reporter scribbled something on the pad and then continued. "Okay. Do you know that those same two students that you suspended have both disappeared?" Harold looked shocked at this. He assumed that Homer had made it home safely. "I do not know anything about that." The reporter wrote some more on his pad, then he looked up at him. "So, you're telling me that you can neither confirm nor deny that you suspended two students yesterday, and as of last night, both of them have been reported missing, and then this morning you find that message painted on your sidewalk." Harold could feel his blood boiling, he did not like where this was going. "And so the big question is, are you going to cancel the prom this Friday night?" Harold stood to his feet, feeling rage build up inside of him, he pointed to the door. "I am not answering any of your questions, there is the door, don't let it hit on the ass on your way out." The reporter wrote one more thing down on his pad, then replaced them in his shirt pocket. "Well, there is no need to get hostile Mr. Payne, or would you rather me call you Harold?" Harold pointed to the door again. "Would you just get out of here.", he demanded, and with that, the reporter took his leave. Before he walked through the door he turned and smiled at him. "You gave me more answers than you realize." Harold picked up a paperweight off of his desk and poised himself to throw it at the reporter. "Touchy!" the reporter said, then left, closing the door behind him. Harold let out a deep breath and sat the paperweight back on his desk, looking around the room he felt defeated. He sat back down, put his head in his palms, then melted into his chair.

Sara sat on one of the park benches that sat on the patio just outside of the cafeteria. Jerry spotted her and walked over to where she was sitting. She looked up from a book she was reading and smiled at him. He sat next to her and put his hand on her shoulder. "Good morning." he said as he kissed her on the cheek. "Hi." She smiled at him and then gently kissed him on the lips. She really cared for him, he always seemed so genuine with his feelings for her. "Have you heard about the message this morning?" She looked at him, confusion on her face. "What message?" "Well, I know they are trying to clean it up, but someone painted a message on the sidewalk up by the office this morning, it was some kind of poem about cancelling the prom." "How do you know?" She asked. "I needed to come early this morning, I am helping to repaint the boy's gym for next year, and I saw the police here. I tried to hear what it was all about, but I couldn't hear anything. Anyway, I do know that they are not going to cancel the prom regardless of the threat." "So that is why you were not at the bus stop this morning." He shook his head yes, then kissed her on the cheek again. "Have you seen Homer this morning?" she asked, he was not at the bus stop either. "Oh," he said, "I heard he was suspended yesterday after lunch. I guess he took off and no one has seen him since." She looked concerned, closed her book, and sat it on the bench. "For what?" she asked, her eyes meeting his. "I am not sure, something about some weed they found in his locker." Jerry looked at her, she appeared really upset at this news. "Where did you hear that from?" Her voice had changed, getting angrier as she talked. "I heard it from John, he told me yesterday during seventh period." She looked cross at him, he sat back, this was not his fault, he thought. "How in the hell did he know?" He shook his head, "I don't know, I just know he told me that it happened after lunch." "Why didn't you tell me last night?" "I didn't think it was that important." He stood up from the bench. "Geesh, sometimes I just don't understand you. You said you don't like Homer, yet you are worried about him, what gives?" She looked at him, he noticed a change on her face, like there was more compassion than anger. "I have known him a long time, and he has been picked on so much, I just worry about him and want him to be safe." Jerry did not expect this answer and he changed his tone, "I totally understand that. I don't like that they pick on him so much either. I mean, he is not a bad guy, just a little nerdy. But hey, who isn't" He smiled and patted her on the head. She looked up at him and smiled. She stood up from the bench and looked at her watch. "Hey, it's almost time for first period, want to walk me to class?" He smiled, "Thought you would never ask." He picked up her books and stuck them under his left arm, then took her hand. Together they walked away.

John stood outside the video game arcade that stood across the street from the high school. He kept looking at his watch then looking around. It was already five past eight and first period was going to be starting in a few minutes. He looked around again when he saw Sheila. She was heading his way. Did Doug change his mind, he thought. He slicked back his hair and straightened his shirt. "He John." she said as she approached him. He put his hand in front of his mouth, breathed into it, then sniffed it to see if his breath smelled okay. He smiled at her, "Hi." She stood in front of him then smiled. "Have you seen Doug?" He frowned, "No, I was supposed to meet him here this morning before school, but he has not shown up yet." She looked at her watch. "Yeah, that shit head was supposed to call me last night, and I never heard from him." What an ass, John thought. "I have not talked to him since last night either, I just know he was supposed to meet me here, said he had something for me." She gave him a funny look, "Like what?" "Well, he was going to pay me for what I did for him yesterday." She gave him another funny look. He looked at her, she was pretty to him, he thought, but not as pretty as Mrs. Hollingsworth, although he did like her hair. Her hair was almost down to her waist and was dirty blond in color. "What did you do?" He did not mind telling her, Doug would tell her anyway. "So, you know that asshole that got Doug suspended yesterday, well, I planted some weed in his locker so he would get suspended too." She looked at him, then she began laughing. "You mean Homer? What an idiot. So you are the one who put the weed in his locker?" He started laughing, "Yeah, but hey," he stopped laughing, "don't tell anyone," She looked at him, she could hardly stop laughing herself, it was about time someone took care of that weasel, she thought. "Don't worry, I won't say a word." She looked at her watch and then looked across the street at the high school. "Listen, if Doug shows up, tell him to meet at the Dairy Freeze at lunch okay?" He shook his head, then she turned and headed for the high school. John stood there for a few moments, looked at his watch, then huffed. Doug was not going to show up, he thought. He would catch him later, he thought. What he had not noticed was that there was someone watching and listening to him. They stood in the shadows of the video arcade store just out of sight. They watched as John walked away and headed for the high school.

6

Mrs. Hollinsworth pulled open a drawer on her filing cabinet and riffled through the folders. She was looking for something specific and when she found it, she smiled and pulled it out. The file she took out was marked cupcakes. She closed the drawer and walked over to her desk that sat in the front of the classroom. The classroom door opened, and John walked in. She smiled at him as he closed the door behind him and walked over to her desk. He looked her over carefully. She was wearing a white blouse and a tan skirt that went just past her knees. She looked lovely today, he thought, as he inched closer to her. "So, shouldn't you be at your first class this morning?" He looked down at the file she had sitting on her desk, then looked back at her. "My first period class was canceled this morning." She gave him a stern look, "Canceled?" she asked. He thought as fast as he could to make up something. "Um, yeah. Our regular teacher is sick and they could not get a substitute, so they canceled class." She squinted her eyes, she did not believe him, but gave him the benefit of the doubt. "So then, why are you here?" He looked back down at the file on the desk. "Well, I knew you did not have a class this morning and you mentioned yesterday that starting today all your classes were going to be making cupcakes, so I thought I would come in and help you sort through the recipes." He smiled at her, he thought this up pretty fast, even faster than normal, he thought. He was hoping she would buy it and let him stay. He glanced down at her legs, trying to get a better look at them, then he noticed that she caught him. She smiled, ever so slightly, then cleared her throat. "Sure. Well, actually, you could take these to the library and make some copies for me. That would be a huge help." He frowned. He was hoping that he could stay in the classroom and be with her. Reluctantly, he took the handful of papers she was holding out. "So, there are five different recipes there. I need at least twenty copies of each of those. You got that?" He shook his head yes. "So then, if Mr. Hampton goes looking for you," he smiled slowly faded away,

"I can tell him that I was having you make up some time for me." She smiled at him. "You see, I saw him this morning in the teachers' lounge, and he looked just fine to me." How did she know that he was his first period teacher, he wondered. That didn't matter, he thought, he got to see her anyway. "Okay, I will be back in just a little bit with your copies." He smiled at her, she smiled back, then he headed out of the room.

She watched as John left the classroom, settling back in her chair, she began to grade papers from the previous day. Her phone rang, she looked at it like she was terribly annoyed. She picked up the receiver and placed it against her ear. "Hello." There was silence on the other end. Feeling a bit irritated, she said it again. There was still no answer, this made her furious. "Listen, if you don't answer me this very moment, I will hang up on you." She listened carefully; she could hear breathing on the other end. "Listen, I know this is a closed line and you can only call from the office or another classroom, so whoever this is, I do not think this is one bit funny." With that, she hung up the phone, stood from her desk, and walked to the door. She opened it ever so slightly and peered outside. She looked in both directions and did not see anyone. She stepped back and let the door close. This was ridiculous, she thought. She heard a sound coming from behind the filing cabinets. She knew she was in here alone, but she wondered what could have made that noise. As she approached, she heard it again. It sounded like someone had just leaned up against the back of one of the cabinets and it popped. She stopped at this and decided that if she was going to take a look, she was going to be more cautious. Even though it was against school policy, she had a can of mace in her purse. She felt that if anyone ever tried anything with her, she would have protection. As quietly as she could, she turned and headed towards her desk where her purse was hanging on her chair. She walked as slow as she could, tiptoeing across the room. She almost made it to her desk, when suddenly a gloved hand clasped over her mouth, preventing her from screaming.

John smiled as he walked down the corridors of the high school, heading towards the library. He thought about how he and Mrs. Hollingsworth could run away together. She was the perfect woman, he thought. He could make her happy and give her everything she ever needed. He thought about her legs and how he was able to see them while she was sitting at her desk. He thought she was the most beautiful woman in the world, and he could see her as his wife. He approached the library and saw a bulletin on the door. He stopped to read it. Huge book sale and history of the civil war display. That sounded interesting, he thought. He continued reading, see a part of history from uniforms to muskets, photographs, and books. He raised his eyebrows, muskets, he thought, those would be cool to look at, he thought. He was going to have to check this out before prom. He opened the door and entered the library then sashayed up to the counter then looked around for the librarian. When he did not see her, he walked around the counter into the main hall of the library and looked around to see if she was putting books away. He walked down each aisle looking for her, and when he reached the fiction section, he saw her. "Hello Mrs. Fredricks, I need to make some copies for Mrs. Hollingsworth, can I have a key to the copy room?" She looked at him over her glasses and smiled. "Sure." she said, then she shelved the book she had in her hand and then headed towards the counter. "So, the display sounds exciting." She glanced over at him and smiled again. "Yes, it is the first time we have had this one here. We are pretty excited about it too. Are you going to come and check it out?' "Oh yeah, I figured I would come and look at everything before prom." "That seems to be the consensus among everyone else too." When they reached the counter, she went behind it and opened a drawer. She held out a key on a chain and John took it gingerly. He smiled at her then walked over to a locked door on the opposite side of the counter. This door opened up into the copy room, He unlocked the door and walked in, turned on the light, then headed for one of the many copy machines that were lined up on the left side wall. As he made his copies, he daydreamed about what it would be like to be married to her. Then he thought about the sex, that would be great, he thought. He fantasized about how he would make love to her. He wanted it to be romantic, to give it to her like no one else had. He noticed that something was happening to his nether region and decided that he needed to think about something else. He started thinking about the civil war display instead. Those muskets will be so awesome to look at, he thought. Then he began to wonder if they would allow people to hold them. He looked down and noticed that he was not standing at attention any longer and he breathed a sigh of relief. The room he was in had windows all along the left wall that looked out into the library over the bank of copy machines. He looked out to see if there was anyone in the library that might have been watching him. He wiped the sweat from his forehead as he noticed that there was no one else there. He continued making copies until he had finished all of them. When he finished, he cleaned everything up, put all of the copies in a large stack, turned out the light, locked the door, and closed it behind him. He walked over to the counter and handed the key back to the librarian, she smiled, and then he left.

On his way back to the classroom, he thought about how he could tell Mrs. Hollingsworth how much he was in love with her. Yes, she was much older than he was, but only by about fifteen years, that would be okay. When he reached the classroom, he opened the door and realized the lights were off. "Hello?" he said. There was no answer. He reached over and flipped on the lights then walked in and closed the door. He moved in a little further into the room and called out again. "Mrs. Hollingsworth, are you in here?" There was still no answer. He shrugged his shoulders and walked through the classroom to the front where her desk was. He looked around and wondered where she might have gone. He looked around towards the back of the room where washers and dryers were. There was also a row of filing cabinets that were in front of them. He started to walk back there, then realized that would be senseless, if she was behind the file cabinets, why would the lights be off. He looked at her desk, her purse was hanging on the back of her chair, so she must not have gone very far. He shrugged again then decided that he would go to one of the kitchens and lay out the papers on one of the counters. He could separate them by their recipe, and this would make it easier for her to pass out. Turning his back to the door, he began to separate the recipes. He began humming to himself as he worked. He did not notice the classroom door slowly open as someone stepped in. Standing there watching John separate the recipes, the person slowly began to walk towards them. John continued to hum while he worked and did not know that anyone had entered the room. Walking silently, the person came upon him slowly, not making any noise, the person stopped directly behind him. John stopped humming and slowly sat down the papers he was working. Sensing that someone was behind him, he quickly turned around. When he saw who was standing there, he smiled, "Oh hi."

7

Miller's office was in disarray at the present moment, and he hated it. He was one of those people who liked everything organized, neat, and tidy. On the wall behind his desk hung a ten-by-ten cork board. Pinned to the board was a picture of Doug, the shed where the blood stain was, and a picture of the graffiti that had been painted on the sidewalk at the high school. Miller was standing over it silently, studying it, trying to connect the dots. There was a knock at the door and Miller turned to see who it was. Bradock was leaning against the door jam, Miller waved him, and he walked over to the board. "I checked out that address you gave, and you know what is strange, it is a small walnut grove. There is not one single house on that lot." Miller looked over at him, a puzzled look on his chiseled face. "I also called the number you gave me, but there was no answer, do you think this boy is missing as well?" Miller looked back over his board, "He might be, what was the report from the lab on that sample we found in the shed?' Bradock held up a report, "It is blood alright, O positive. They ran the sample against the whole family, and it turned out to be Doug's." Miller shook his head, "I think these incidents are related, but I am not sure how." Bradock turned his attention to the board, then back to Miller, "I do have a theory. You said both boys were in an altercation, then they were both suspended. What if they got into another fight and hurt each other?" Miller looked back over him, a surprised look on his face, "That's a good thought, except for one thing, both of them are missing. Where are they, if they hurt each other, wouldn't they have shown up at say a hospital, or even the morgue? I think it is related, but we are way off base, there is something we are missing." Miller leaned back against his desk; he looked back over at the board paying attention to the picture of the graffiti on the sidewalk. "You see this," he pointed to the picture, "there is something else, not it says that one is already gone, and others are lined up." He crossed his arms, a frown crawled across his face, Bradock noticed this change and stepped back. "I believe that if

Mr. Payne does not cancel the prom, we may see more disappearances." Bradock shifted his stance then looked at him squarely, "Unless it is two separate incidents." Miller looked over at him, his face now almost unreadable, "Well now, that's the conundrum then, isn't it?" There was a dead silence in the office as both of them looked at the board again. Miller looked at his watch, it was nearly seven thirty. Where had the time gone, he thought. The deafening silence was broken by the ringing of the telephone, both Miller and Bradock flinched. Miller stood from his leaning position, turning around, he picked up the receiver from its cradle. "Give it to me." Bradock strained to hear what was being said on the other end of the phone, but he could not hear anything. He watched Miller; his face was expressionless. Miller listened carefully, then bent over his desk, grabbing a pen and piece of paper, he jotted something down, hung up the phone, and picked the paper up from his desk. "You know how I said that this could get worse?" Bradock shook his head. "Well, we have another disappearance, here is the address." He handed the note to Bradock, then, picking up his hat and placing it on his head, said, "Let's go."

Miller and Bradock arrived at their destination, pulled up to the curb, and exited the vehicle. "I am going to let you do the talking." Bradock said with a crooked smile. As they approached the house, the front door flung open and a large woman in a blue bathrobe busted through. "Are you the police?" she said as loud as she could. "Yes ma'am." Miller said. "Well, it's about damn time you got here, I called over an hour ago." She was swinging her hands in the air, her hair was a mess, she looked frumpy, Bradock thought. "Listen, my son was supposed to be here right after school." She held up her left foot. "He takes care of my ulcer for me." Bradock and Miller both looked down, she had a large open sore on her heel. Bradock felt his stomach churn as he looked at it. "Well, here it is almost nine at night, and he ain't here." Miller looked back up at her, trying to hide the grin from his face due to her outburst. "When was the last time you saw him?" He pulled out his notepad and pencil. "He left for school this morning; he rides the bus. I can't afford to get him no car!" Bradock raised his eyebrows, this woman was a little off her rocker, he thought. "Has he ever done this before?" She looked down at the ground, then back at the two officers. "Not that I can recall, I mean there are times when he is hanging around that asshole football jock itch son of bitch," she looked as if she was looking for words, like trying to remember something, "what his face, uh, Doug, you know that prick football player." Bradock tried to laugh at her choice of words, then something clicked inside of him. "What is your son's name?" he asked. She looked over at him, "His name is John, what are you, some kind of numb nut? I already told the lady who answered the phone." Miller looked at her squarely, "Your son hangs around with Doug Burton?" She gave him a sharp look, "Isn't that what I just said, geesh, what kind of cops are you?" Miller looked over at Bradock, "Are you thinking what I am thinking?" Bradock shook his head. "Can we see the boys room?" "Follow me." she said, turned, and headed back towards the house. As they walked through the front door, they both noticed a strange order. Miller looked the place over and realized that there were about eight cats littering the living room. This must have been the smell he encountered. She led them down a narrow hallway that took them to two bedrooms, one on either side of the hall. She opened the door and flipped on a light switch, "Here it is, but I don't think you are going to find him in there." She stood by as they walked past her into the room. It was a mess, clothes all over the floor, the bed unmade, and papers strung from one end of the room to the other. "This is a mess." Miller said, "I have never understood how a person could sleep, let alone live, in a mess like this." They looked the room, turning over clothes, and picking through the papers. Bradock found a small plastic bag on the dresser and picked it up, "Looks like marijuana." he said. He pulled an evidence bag from his pants pocket, stuffed the little bag into, closed it up and put it back. When they didn't find anything else, they turned and left the room. "Do you have a list of John's friends or phone numbers to where he might be?' The woman shook her head. "It's just me and John, his frickin father took off about ten years ago, he only has the one friend, and no girlfriends. I don't know where he would be unless he is still at the school." Miller took a card from his shirt pocket and handed it to her. "This is my personal number, if he shows up, please give me a call." She looked at the card then stuffed it into a pocket of her robe. "So that's it huh, you going to give me a brush off just like that. You pigs are all the same, ask you to help and what do you do, look around and then say "call me if he comes home", well what if he is out there bleeding or kidnapped, or worse yet, he has been taken by one of those terrorist groups and turned into some gibbering idiot that wants to take over the world?" Miller looked at her, his voice caring, his expression compassionate, "We are not giving up, we are going to check out the school and follow up with you with anything we find, try not to worry." He smiled at her, she smiled back, and with that, Miller and Bradock left.

As they sat in the car, Bradock looked over at Miller, "Terrorist group?" he said with a chuckle. Miller smiled as he started the vehicle and pulled away from the curb. Bradock looked at him, "So, what are you thinking?" He looked at Miller, but he could not read his face. "There may be a connection there, but we are going to have to check all angles." "Where should we check first?" Bradock asked, he was a little apprehensive asking this question as he thought it was obvious, but he was not sure what Miller was thinking. "I was thinking the high school. Even if we just made a quick tour of the grounds, but I am sure we won't find anything there." "What do you think the connection is?" Miller turned his head slightly and looked at him, his face still unreadable, then he looked back at the road "Well first of all, we have three people missing, no bodies, and only two clues, a small blood stain and the graffiti. Second, for all we know, this could be an elaborate prank, it is not the first time, and I am sure it won't be the last." "A prank?" Miller took a deep breath, "Yes, back in 1954 there was an incident during the prom. It was the day of the prom, there were two students found making out in the school gym earlier that day. Now really that is no big deal, but one of the guys who caught them had been pursuing that same girl for months. So, wanting to get even and pull a prank on them, he got some firecrackers and brought them to the prom. When she was crowned as prom queen, he lit the firecrackers and threw them up on the stage. It startled her and she fell off of the stage, breaking her leg. It nearly killed her, so they stopped the prom for five years just to get everything kind of settled down." Bradock looked at him, he had never heard this story before, and he grew up here. "You said this happened in 1954? That was twenty years ago. I went to Sotterville high, I never heard this story, how do you know about it?" Miller looked at him again, "Because I was the guy who was caught making out with her."

The high school lay silent, completely enveloped by darkness except for a few lights in the main parking lot. Miller and Bradock exited the vehicle and cautiously headed towards the front of the school. Miller took out his flashlight and Bradock followed suit. "This is a huge place; how do you want to do this?" Bradock asked. Miller shone his flashlight from one side, then to the other. "Listen, why don't you take the left and I will take the right, if you see anything, give me a buzz on the walkie talkie. I will do the same. Then let's meet back by the cafeteria." "What about the ag department?" Miller thought for a moment, the high school was much bigger now than it used to be and the ag department was on the left side of the school in the back beyond the cafeteria. "I will check it out, that means you have to check beyond the cafeteria as well, the new metal and wood shops on the other side of the boy's gym." Bradock shook his head and then the two departed, each going in a separate direction. As Bradock made his way around the school, he remembered his days here. He hated high school, it was miserable. There were days when he did not even want to get up from his bed to go. During his senior year something changed. He was enrolled in a self-defense class, one that is no longer offered due to some budget cuts. It made him realize what he wanted to do with his life. He always wanted to help those who could not help themselves, and this was the main reason he went to the police academy after a four-year stint in the Army. He served as an MP while he was stationed at Fort Brag, this helped to concrete his love of policing. While he was at the academy, he wanted to work as hard as he could, this led to him graduating with honors. He was so happy when he earned his position on the police force in his old hometown. He had been on the force now for almost ten years and in that time, he went from patrol to detective. His goal was to be chief of police someday, and that was what he was really working towards. This was not the first time he had worked on a case like this. One of the first cases he worked on as a detective involved a man who had been reported missing. While working on the case he discovered that the man was murdered by his dealer for a bad drug deal that had gone down. The dealer murdered him and then took up to the lake, weighted him down, and tied him to an old fishing weir. He had a horrible thought, he hoped that this did not turn out to be like that case. He continued to look over the grounds, shining his light in every classroom that had an uncovered window. There were a couple of times that he thought he saw something, like a lump that was a pile of coats, and something that looked like a person slumbered over a garbage can, but that turned out to be a garbage bag full of old furniture stuffing from some chair. After looking everywhere, he could see, he finally gave up. He never heard from Miller, so he came to the conclusion that he did not find anything either. He began to head towards the spot where they were supposed to meet and as he approached the cafeteria, he saw Miller sitting on one of the park benches. "I didn't find anything." Miller looked over at him, his face unreadable, "Neither did I, just as I thought. Let's get back to the station and file our reports, then we will pick it up in the morning. I think we should come here first thing and find out if there was any connection with John in the altercation with the other two students." As they walked back to the front of the school, a pair of eyes hiding in the darkness watched them.

8

Harold sat at the table staring down at his bacon and eggs, he really had no appetite, and furthermore, he did not want to go to work today. The last two days had been a nightmare. He picked up his cup of coffee, took a huge swig, and sat it back down. "What's wrong?" his wife asked. He looked up at her. She was still a beautiful woman, standing there in her pink bathrobe, hair up in curlers, and a cigarette hanging out of her mouth. He wished she would quit smoking, but she just could not give it up. They had been married for twelve years, never had any children, and this was just fine with him. He had been a teacher for seven years before he became the principal at the high school for the last four years. He had been married before while he was in college, but that was a rushed and senseless marriage. He had known her since high school and was eager to marry her as soon as he finished community college. As soon as he began at the university, he asked her to marry him and they ran off to Vegas to elope. His parents never liked her, he didn't care. After two years of marriage and going to college, nothing was working. They both decided it was over and parted ways. He met Karen, his new wife, a year later. They fell in love and when he graduated, they were married. While he was teaching grade school, he discovered that he really did not want any children of his own and really hated watching other people's children. Karen was okay with it at first, and the first ten years they were very happy. Then one day she approached him and told him she wanted children of her own. That was when the trouble started. They had drifted apart because of it. Things were not terrible, but he began seeing Darla, who did not want any children either, so he had been planning on getting a divorce. "You have hardly touched your breakfast Harold, what is wrong?" He sighed heavily and took another drink of his coffee. "It has to do with those two boys who are missing. As of yesterday, there was still no sign of them and the police still have no leads or clues. It is three days away from the prom and I just don't want to even go in today." She walked over to him and placed her hand on his shoulder. "Try not to worry dear, they will find them, and everything will be okay." He put his hand on hers and smiled at her. "I really want to believe that Karen, but I just don't know, it has been two days, I mean, what if something really bad happened to them?" "You just have to believe that they are okay and go from there, I am sure the police will find them, I hear this detective Miller is a real hound dog." He shook his head, "Well I have no idea about that, but let's hope he finds them." The phone rang and Karen walked over to where it hung on the wall and answered it. "Hello." she said. Her face instantly turned red as she looked over towards Harold. "It's Darla, for you." Harold pushed himself away from the table, stood up, then walked over to her. Taking the receiver from her, she shot him a look of disgust. Did she know, he thought. "Hello." he said, watching Karen as she went to take his plate off the table. "What's wrong?" he asked. "You better get down here quick, there is another message on the sidewalk about the prom, listen, it is bad, I am calling the police." "No, don't call the police, I will handle it." Karen looked over sharply at him. "No Harold." her voice shaky, "I need to, it talks about murder, I am calling them now." Harold hung the phone up and turned his attention towards Karen, who now looked concerned. "What's going on?" she asked. "There is another message at the school, Darla said it mentions murder." He looked at his watch, it was only 7:00, he rushed over to the table where his briefcase was laying. "I don't have time for breakfast, I will grab something later." She nodded her head, "Listen, just take care, and let the police handle this." He kissed her on the cheek, picked up the case, then headed out the door. If he was going to get there before the police did, he would have to rush.

At the bus stop, Sara was in an embrace with Jerry. Her head was snuggled into his chest. This was her favorite place to be, she thought. He stood about three six inches taller than her, so it was easy for him to rest his chin on her head. She looked up at him and they kissed gently. "Have you heard from Doug?" she asked. He had a confused look on his face, she had just kissed him, then asked about Doug, he wondered. "Um, nope. I have not talked to him since Monday. Why?" "I was just wondering how he was liking his suspension." Jerry smiled, "Oh, I am sure he is having the time of his life. Not having to go to school and just sitting in his room playing his video game." He had always been a little jealous of Doug's video game system. He wanted one for himself but never had the money to buy one. His parents also refused to buy him one as well. He stroked her hair, it was so soft, then put his hand on her cheek, held her close, then kissed her again. He loved the way her soft lips felt against his. He wanted more though, to make love to her would be the most fantastic thing. She would not allow him though, so he settled for kissing and the occasional touch of her breast. He had tried to make love to her only a couple of times, but she told him she wanted to save herself for marriage. He really loved her, so he respected her wishes. They had talked about marriage a few times and decided that after graduation they would decide. He really did not want to rush into anything and neither did she. He had never been with a woman before in that way, and he felt that waiting for Sara was more worth it than anything else in the world. They continued to hug each other until they heard the whining of the approaching bus. They looked deep into each other's eyes for only a moment, he could see just how much she loved him. He had only had two other girlfriends before, but he never felt about them the way he felt about Sara. As Jerry was boarding the bus, he looked around for John. He did not see him anywhere. He took a seat next to Sara and turned to her. "That is strange." She looked up and met his gaze, her eyes looking as lovely as ever. Her voice was soft when she spoke, "What is?" "I was going to ask John if he had seen Doug, but he is not here. He never misses school. He is kind of a nerd like that." She smiled at him, her eyes seemed to twinkle. "Maybe he is already at school." Jerry shook his head, "I don't know, something just doesn't feel right. I have a bad feeling in my gut." She took his hand then smiled at him again. He found comfort in her smile, yet he could not shake this feeling that something was wrong. "Well, then I will look for him when we get there." As they approached the school, Jerry saw that there were two police cars, a news van, and a large crowd around the admin office. "I wonder what is going on this time?" Sara looked out the window, then shrugged her shoulders. When the bus came to a stop, Jerry stood to his feet, feeling very anxious as he could hardly wait to exit. When they got off of the bus he took Sara by the hand, then lef her to the front of the school where all the excitement seemed to be happening.

Detective Miller stood next to Mr. Payne as they both looked down at the message scrawled in red paint on the sidewalk. There was a crime scene photographer taking photos, and a forensics analyst collecting samples of the paint. Darla stood on the opposite side of Mr. Payne; she could feel her body trembling. There was no doubt about it, she was frightened. She had never seen anything like this before, and now two days in a row. She looked at the message again.

"You did not listen, now two are dead. Stop the prom, or you will lose your head."

She thought surely that this was no longer a prank but a real threat. Miller looked over at Mr. Payne and noticed his face was pale. "Maybe we better talk in your office." Payne turned to him; he had a feeling like a steel ball had fell in his gut. He shook his head and they both turned towards the office. He looked back at Darla; she looked as if she had seen a ghost. When he spoke to her, it was as gentle as he could. "Stay here, answer any questions, and assist in any way you can." She nodded, even though she did not feel like talking to anyone, she felt she needed to be as professional as possible. He smiled at her, and she faintly smiled back as she watched the two of them disappear into the building.

Sara felt like Jerry was pulling her as they rushed along the hallway to get to the front of the school. When Jerry reached the crowd he stopped suddenly, Sara crashing into him. "Wait here." he said, "I am going to take a closer look." She nodded and with that, Jerry pushed his way to the front of the crowd of students that had been gathered around the message. As he read it, he could feel the blood drain from his face, a knot forming in his stomach, then he suddenly felt sick as if he was going to vomit. He turned away from the message on the sidewalk and moved slowly back to where he had left Sara. When she saw him she could see that his face looked pale. She clasped her arms around him and his head sunk deep into her chest. She placed a hand on his head and gently stroked his hair. In a soft voice, she whispered in his ear, "What is it?" He looked up at her, his mouth trying to form words, but nothing came out. He had that feeling of comfort again. He could feel her breasts on his cheek as she held him in her arms. He hesitated to pull away from her, and even though he did not want to, he needed to face her. "There is another message." he said, concern in his voice this time, "It says that there are two people dead." She looked at him, she noticed the color returning to his face as he became more aware of himself. "I have a really bad feeling, both Doug and John are missing, and I have not heard from either one of them since Monday." He had a horrible thought in the back of his mind and he did not know how to say it. Deep down he knew how Sara felt about Homer, but what if she was wrong, what if deep down Homer was not as nice as she thought. He looked at her again, and even though he tried to be as calm about it as he could, it came pouring out. "If they are dead, and someone killed them, it had to be Homer." She looked at him and he could see the fire glowing in her eyes. "What do you mean?" she said. "Doug and John played the horrible trick on Homer on the bus Monday, since then, no one has seen any of them. You yourself said that you had not seen Homer since then either. It only makes sense." She burst into laughter. Jerry was confused, how could she laugh at this. "What, why are you laughing?" She put her hand on his shoulder and looked him squarely in the face. "You sound like this is one of those cheesy slasher movies that we go and watch at the drive in. I mean come on, you are talking about two of your best friends and a kid who is mostly afraid of his own shadow. Yes, I like Homer, but murder? He couldn't even dissect a frog in biology class." She shook her head at him and he suddenly felt very sheepish. "It is a great theory and all, but I still think someone is pulling Mr. Payne's chain." He let out a sigh and rubbed his eyes. "I guess you are right, it does seem kind of silly." He took her hand as they headed back towards the school.

Detective Miller sat in the chair opposite Mr. Payne. He had already taken out his notepad and pencil and was jotting down a few notes. "Listen Mr. Payne, I am going to be honest with you. That message may or may not be legitimate, but we cannot ignore the facts anymore. I have two reports of students who are missing, Doug Burton and John Templan. And that brings up another fact, that address we got from your secretary for Homer Fenstra turned out to be a bust as well. It was a walnut grove. No one ever answers the phone and to my knowledge, this student is missing as well. I would take this as a threat and with that in mind, I think you need to reconsider shutting down the prom." Harold sat forward, laced his fingers together, and when he spoke, he put authority behind his voice. "I have been thinking about this all morning. The missing boys, well, I don't know much about that, but since you have no corpse, you have no clues, and you do not have suspects I think that the whole thing is a farce and to my knowledge it is not the first one this school has ever had. With that in mind, I will tell you one more time, the prom will not be canceled. Now if you feel that there is a real threat, then you do what you need to do to protect everyone. Bring in police, bring in guards, bring in the fricken SWAT team if you want, but let me assure you that this Friday night at eight sharp there will be a prom." He sat back in his chair, folded his arms, and did not budge. Miller stood up from his chair, put his pencil and pad back in his pocket and turned to leave. When he reached the door, he turned back and looked Harold squarely in the face, making sure to give him complete eye contact. "Well Mr. Payne, or Harold, or whatever you want to be called, you can rest assured that we will be watching and if anything else happens, it will fall on your shoulders and then, you will know that I will hold you responsible. You have been warned sir." With that he turned and made his exit. Harold sunk into his chair; in the back of his mind, he wondered if he was making a mistake. He picked up his phone and dialed the front desk, "Darla, I need to see you." By the time he hung up the phone she was in his office. She strutted over to his chair and sat in his lap. She put her arms around his neck and gently kissed him on the mouth. His hands felt their way up the curves of her body. She was about to kiss him again when the phone rang. She slipped off of his lap and he slowly answered the phone. "Mr. Payne here." The voice on the other end of the phone was silent, almost whispering and he could barely make out what they were saying. "You want this to end?" the voice said. "Listen," Mr. Payne said, "I can barely hear you." There was a silence on the other end of the phone for a brief moment. When the person spoke again their voice was gruff, "You want this to stop, meet me in the wood shop at noon." There was a click and then silence. A few seconds later he could only hear a dial tone. Harold hung the phone up and looked at Darla. "I think we can put all of this shit behind us." She gave him a quizzical look. "I am not sure who that was on the phone, but I think it is the punk who has been leaving the messages. They want to meet me in the wood shop at noon." "What if there really is a killer and this is a trap?" He smiled as he opened his top desk drawer and pulled out a snub nosed .38. Darla looked down at the gun he now held in his hand and nearly gasped. "Have you had that the whole time?" He looked at her with a smile still on his face. "This is a tough job and you never know when you will have to protect yourself from any thugs." She put her hands on his shoulders and began rubbing his neck. "Oh, you are so sexy, I want you right now." she said in a sultry voice. He sat the gun on the desk, stood up, then swept her in his arms. As he bent down to kiss her again, he looked over at the gun, "I dare that little punk to try something." with that, he kissed her again.

Detective Miller stood outside the office looking at the message that was scrawled out on the sidewalk. Bradock walked up to him and nudged his arm. "Tell me something." Bradock pulled a piece of paper out of his back pocket and unfolded it. "I have the analysis from the first message. It was paint, just like we thought, but there is something else." Miller looked over at him, "What else could be there?" he asked. Bradock took a deep breath and exhaled. "Are you ready for this?" Miller shot him a glance that seemed to say "just shut up and tell me". Bradock smiled and then continued. "There was blood mixed in with the paint, just a minute amount, but it was enough to give it that tint of red it had. But here is the kicker Miller, it matched the blood stain we found in the Burton's shed." Miller turned to him, once again his face unreadable. "Do you know what that means? It means this went from just a missing persons case to possible homicide." Bradock nodded in agreement. Miller waved his hand around as he spoke. "I have tried to get the principal here to cancel the prom and he will not do it." "Can we get a court order?" Miller shook his head no, "Not with what we have. What we need is to find one of the three missing students, if we had a corpse, it would really help. All we have right now is circumstantial evidence and no judge is going to sign off on that. No Bradock, we need to broaden our search and find a dead body."

9

Jerry had volunteered to work in the school library for an hour every day. He enjoyed doing this kind of work and had even thought about going to college to be a librarian. He took a lot of ribbing from his fellow basketball players because of this being called a geek or even a book nerd, but he did not care. He walked through the back office looking at the boxes that were being unpacked for the Civil War display that was going to be starting over the next day or so. He was hoping they could get the display up by this afternoon. This would give all the students the chance to come in and see everything. He began unpacking the boxes when the librarian walked up to him. "What do you think you are doing young man?" Mrs. Fredricks asked. He stood up sharply and noticed that she had been standing over him, watching him silently. He smiled faintly and when he spoke, his voice cracked. "Um, er, I thought I would start unpacking these and get them ready for the display." Why did he just talk like that, he thought? He looked at her again and noticed a small smile creep across her face. "Well, honestly, let's wait. The college is sending over an instructor. I guess he is the expert in this field and has a way that he wants it all set up. So, we will leave that to him." She looked over at the stack of boxes in the corner. These were the books for the book sale they were going to be having. "Why don't you take those out and process them, get them ready for the sale on Friday." He sighed, he really wanted to look at the Civil War memorabilia, guess it would have to wait he thought. She smiled and turned to leave to let him work on the boxes. He looked over at them, there were at least ten boxes full of books. He sighed again and began to walk over to them when he saw Sara walk in, he smiled at her and she smiled back. She walked around the counter to where he was standing, and they fell into each other's arms in an embrace. It only lasted for a few moments as Sara caught a glimpse of Mrs. Fredricks and she cut the hug short. "Have you heard anything more?" he asked. "She shook her head no, "Not a thing. After the police left the janitor cleaned the sidewalk off. That was it." He looked down at the ground. "Do you think we have anything to be worried about?" She smiled, her eyes looking deep into his and he smiled back. "I don't think we have anything to worry about." He took her hand, "So then, do you think the prom is still on?" She shrugged her shoulders, "As far as I know they are not canceling it. So yeah, it is still on." He smiled again. "I will pick you up at five-thirty so we can grab a little dinner before." Jerry looked down at his watch, it was eleven-thirty, he only had a half an hour left before lunch. "I am so glad you came to see me, but how did you get out of class?" Jerry asked. She smiled and let out a giggle, "I have a hall pass to go to the bathroom." "So you came here to see me, you little sneak." She kissed him on the cheek, smiled again, then turned to leave. He watched her as she walked back through the library on her way to the door. Deep down inside he felt that she was the one that he wanted to spend the rest of his life with. He looked back over at the stack of boxes and sighed again.

Harold picked up the snub nosed thirty-eight from his desk, opened it to make sure it was loaded, then stuffed it into his pants pocket. If someone was going to threaten him, he was going to be ready. He walked over to his door and opened it slightly. As he peered through the crack, he could see Darla sitting at her desk. He opened it wide enough to motion for her. She looked over and saw him, rose from her desk, and walked to where he was standing. "I want to see you for just a moment." he said and pulled her into his office. When he shut the door behind her, he grabbed her and held her close. She kissed him gently on the lips. "When?" she asked. He knew what she was talking about. He had promised her that as soon as this school year was over, he was going to divorce his wife and marry her. He held her close, and their eyes met. It was like he could see deep into her soul. "As soon as the school year is over. I have already filed the paperwork with the lawyer." She smiled, held him in an embrace. She pressed her lips to his in a passionate kiss. She reached up and took his hair in her hands pulling it slightly. He put his hands on her back and slowly moved them down, feeling every curve of her body. They backed up against the door causing a loud thud. She did not care, thrusting her body against his. He kissed her again, then gently pushed her away. She looked at him, puzzled as to why he would stop. He looked over at the clock on the wall, it read eleven forty-five. She followed his glance and when she saw the time, she understood. She gently kissed him on the cheek. "Don't take any crap and come back in one piece." He patted the bulge that was in the waistline of his pants where he had placed his handgun. "I got all the protection I need to be safe right here." She glanced down at his crotch and smiled. He looked at her squarely in the face, "No matter what though, no matter what happens, you make sure the prom goes on just as planned. I will not let the students down, they have waited all year for this." She smiled, "What could possibly happen?" He shook his head, "I don't know, but you are in charge." He turned around and opened the door, then looked back at her as if he forgot something. "Oh, I almost forgot, I have a meeting this afternoon with my lawyer and may not be back after lunch." She nodded, this meant that she would be in charge since the high school did not have a vice principal at this time. Darla went out first and he followed. As he walked out of the office, he turned and looked at her again. She smiled and blew him a kiss.

As he walked through the school on his way to the woodshop in the back, he thought about who he was going to be seeing and just what their angle was. He thought that maybe it was Doug and that he was trying to get even with him for the suspension he gave him. As he passed by the different classrooms, he would peer in to make sure classes were underway. It would be lunch time soon and all of the classes would be vacant except for some of those teachers that stayed and ate lunch in their rooms while they graded papers or prepared for their next class. He knew that he was not going to let anyone ruin the prom. He also knew that Darla would make sure it would be the greatest prom the school ever had. When he approached the woodshop, he noticed that the lights were off. He was under the impression that there would be a class going on at this time. He opened the door cautiously and peered inside. "Hello?" There was no answer. Maybe the person he was meeting, which he was sure was Doug, was not here yet. He smiled, this gave him the element of surprise. He entered through the door and it slowly shut behind him. This made him jump and he turned to look at the door, there was no one there. "No time to get jumpy." he said to himself. He looked around the room, it was cast with shadows from the light coming through the window of the door. He noticed that the shades were pulled shut on all the other windows in the classroom and this made it even darker inside. As he scanned the classroom, he noticed that there were various saws around the room, including what looked like a table saw. He made his way through the room, heading towards the front where the teacher's desk would normally be. Suddenly he heard one of the saws come on. It made a loud buzzing noise. He jerked around to see which one it was, it was too dark to make out. "Glad you could make it, right on time." The voice seemed to come from nowhere. He looked around the room, but he could not see anyone. He reached into his waistband and retrieved his revolver. "Listen up Doug, I am not going to fall for any of your crap, you better turn on the lights and show yourself." There was no answer. Harold began to stumble around the room, his revolver in the ready position. "Listen here punk, I know you are angry that I suspended you, but you should know I have a gun, and I am not afraid to use it." He held the gun up as if to show it off to whoever was talking. The person spoke again, Harold tried to identify the voice, but it sounded like the person was holding their hand over their face, muffling their voice. "So you think this is Doug? You are wrong. So tell me, are you going to stop the prom?" Harold stood there for a moment, listening to the sound of the saw running in the background, trying desperately to identify the voice. "Not on your life pal." he said, moving from side to side. Another saw was turned on from the opposite side of the room. Harold flinched and turned around, waving his gun. "Show yourself punk, let me see your face." He moved through the classroom, checking each saw as we went. When he came to the first saw that was running, he shut it off. The voice spoke again, "Now why did you do that, you are spoiling my fun. Cancel the prom and all this will stop." Harold turned, he thought he found where the voice was coming from, turning off the one saw made it a little quieter. "I am not stopping the prom because you, Doug." He moved towards the far-right side of the room where he thought he heard the voice coming from. Another saw was turned on on the left side of the room and Harold stopped dead in his tracks. He lifted his gun again and turned towards the sound. "If you are not Doug, then who are you?" There was no answer. He turned again. From behind him, a hand covered with a black glove reached around and covered his face. From outside of the woodshop the saws could barely be heard. There was a single gunshot that rang through the classroom. The saws were shut off, and all was quiet.

10

Bradock looked over at the clock on the wall, it read six fifteen. He didn't like this time of the night, it was still almost one hundred degrees outside, and it did not feel like the air conditioner in the office was working well at all. He had not seen Detective Miller since earlier that day, and he wanted to share some information with him. He was standing in Millers' office studying the crime scene photos from the school and the Burton's shed that Miller had on his corkboard. He looked at the picture of the blood stain on the floor, then back over at the picture of the first message from the high school sidewalk. He picked up a report from the desk and looked it over. This was the report about John Templen who had gone missing on Tuesday. On the cork board there was a picture of Doug, John, and a picture of Homer that he had received from the high school. He was still puzzled over Homer Fenstra and the fact that there was no other information about him. He had tried to dig into the students' past and he had discovered that before high school, there was no record of him anywhere. He even checked with local databases and state records and did not even find a birth certificate. This did not seem possible to him, so he began to conduct a full investigation. He completed interviews with his teachers and other staff from the high school. They had nothing bad to say about the boy, other than he was an introvert, bullied by other students, and spent a lot of time to himself. He had excellent grades, was never late, and never was in trouble or even missed a day of school. They were all shocked when they found out that he had drugs in his locker and was suspended for the final week of school. This led him to do a thorough search of Homer's locker. There were no other traces of drugs, and he found no evidence to support the claim that he had been selling them. They took a sample of his fingerprints and submitted them to the local database, but it turned up nothing. It was like this kid had never existed before high school. All of this led back to the altercation and subsequent suspension of both Doug and Homer. Through his research he discovered that later that same day, an unknown person called the school and reported that Homer had sold him a fair amount of Marijuana. When they opened his locker, they found a bag that contained almost two ounces. He had taken the bag and entered it into evidence, and it was sitting on the desk. He continued to puzzle over this when the desk sergeant knocked on the door. "Excuse me Lieutenant, but the Burton's are here, and they want to talk to you." Bradock turned to him, "Okay, I will be out in a moment." He turned back towards the board. Where are you, he thought, and where was Miller?

As he approached the couple in the lobby, he noticed that the mother was crying. She held a neckerchief in her right hand that she had been using to dry her tears, her husband holding her left hand. When the husband looked up and saw him coming, he stood to his feet. "Well, what have you been doing to find my son, it has been three days?" He lurched towards Bradock as if he was going to grab him by the throat. Bradock stepped back, he knew this was not going to be easy, but he had to tell them what he knew. "First of all, we are doing everything we can to find him. We have opened a full investigation into this." Doug's father cut him off, "Listen flathead, don't try and weave your, we are doing everything bullshit. We have been waiting and we have not heard a damn thing, we want to know what you are doing?" Bradock took a slow deep breath, "We have been checking with his friends, his teachers, and any other possible places he may have gone. So far we have turned up nothing. We also put out an A.P.P. to check the bus station, the airport, and any other means of leaving the city. We have also sent his picture to all neighboring law enforcement and the FBI. We have checked with relatives, so please, leave this to us as we are doing everything possible." Doug's father took a step back, "You believe he ran away?" His voice faltered; he was stunned by this news. "Do you have any idea why he would want to run away? Are there troubles at home?" With this question, Doug's father had a scowl that

crawled across his face, "Are you accusing me of something?" Bradock
shook his head no, "Not at all, I am looking at all angels Mr. Burton,
I want to find your son as much as you do, which brings me to my
next question, do you know Homer Fenstra, and did you son have any
contact with him outside of school?" Burton thought about this for
a moment, he looked over at his wife who had seemed to have not
been paying attention to the whole conversation. Then his eyes lit up,
"Yes, as a matter of fact I do know this kid, he is the one responsible
for Doug being put on suspension, did he do something to Doug?"
Bradock held up his hand, "No, it is just that he is missing too, and we
do not have much information on him." Doug's father raised his fist, "If
that brat did anything to my son, so help me." "Mr. Burton," Bradock
said, cutting him off mid-sentence, "there is no evidence of anything
like that. Just rest assured that he will find him." The door to the lobby
opened and Detective Miller stepped in. He assessed the situation and
walked over to the couple. "I see you have come here for some answers,
I am sure that Lieutenant Bradock has answered all your questions?"
Doug's father shook his head then looked towards Bradock, "He told
me everything you are all doing to find my son." "Good." Miller said,
then he took Bradock by the arm and led him back to his office, leaving
the couple by themselves.

They entered and Miller closed the door. "I got some more
information about Homer Fenstra." Bradock licked his lips, this was
what he had been waiting for. Miller sat at his desk and pulled a piece
of paper out of his inside coat pocket. As he unfolded it, Bradock
sat down. "So, the reason that we have not been able to find any
information about Homer Fenstra is that about five years ago, he was
put into protective custody as part of a family dispute." He handed the
paper to Bradock, it was a facsimile from the FBI. "He was a witness
to a horrible crime committed by his father back in 1978. Seems that
his mother had been having an affair and when the father found out
about it, he butchered the man right in front of the boy. Stabbed his

eighteen times in the chest. Homer was taken into custody and was a ward of the state. A few months later, he was adopted and moved here, but he and his new family are under assumed names, and their location is hidden from prying eyes. Seems that the father was released a couple of years later, some kind of mistrial, and the new family was hidden as Homer was a key witness to the homicide. The FBI has spoken with the family about the situation and gave me their word that the boy is home and is safe. We can remove him from the list." Bradock thought about it for a moment, then added, "But if was witness to such a horrific crime, and somehow it resonated with him that this is how you deal with things, wouldn't he be a suspect?" Miller sat back in his chair and laced his fingers together, "Except that he has an airtight alibi. He has been home ever since this Monday and has not left the house at all. He has been under supervision the whole time." Bradock sat back in his chair and in the back of his mind, felt a little more at ease. "What about John, we still have nothing on him." Miller smiled, "Oh that is where we have both been misled. Doug and John have been best friends since grade school. I believe that one, if not both, are responsible for putting the Marijuana in Homer's locker." Bradock sat forward and put his hands on Miller's desk, "What?" He had a confused look on his face. "Miller smiled, "After spending some time at the school this afternoon, I met with Darla, the secretary who took the phone call. At first, she was not sure who the person was that made the call. She remembered that the call took place right after lunch, just before sixth period. So we looked at all the attendance records for that day, and John missed his sixth period class, however; he made it to his seventh period class and had no explanation for why he missed the one directly after lunch. Furthermore, I decided to check out the fast-food restaurants and the video game arcade across the street and found that he was spotted using the payphone at the Dairy Freeze ten minutes before one. So, I located the phone booth and took the number and as we speak I am having that number crossed checked with the schools numbers, five will get you ten that we find a match. If I am right, then I believe that Doug and John set this whole thing into motion, and that right now they are both together somewhere laughing at us, the school, and everyone else. Also, we have no corpse." Bradock thought about that for a moment, "What about the blood that was mixed in with the paint, it was Burton's blood." Miller took a moment, then leaned forward into his desk. He looked at Bradock squarely, there seemed to be a twinkle in his eyes when he spoke again. "I was wondering when you were going to bring that up. I thought about that also, so I checked with the lab, and they said that there was only a minuscule amount, not enough to really say that anyone had used a whole pint or more of Doug's blood in the paint. No, I think what we are looking at is a prank gone wrong."

11

Darla pulled into the parking lot of the high school and looked at her watch. It was nearly nine p.m. and yet, it was still daylight out. She had received a phone call at home from Karen. She had asked her to meet her at the high school at nine. She looked around the parking lot and did not see anyone, there were also no other vehicles there. She sighed and looked down. She thought that maybe Harold had finally told her about them and asked for his divorce. She looked around again and noticed that a light in the office was on. She did not understand why she wanted to meet here, but then again, there were a lot of things she did not understand. She opened her car door and stepped out. As she walked to the office, she thought about what she was going to say to Karen. This would be so uncomfortable, but she knew it was going to have to happen sooner or later. When she reached the door, she hesitated before she opened it. "Well, here goes nothing." she said, then opened the door.

As she walked in, she looked around the lobby and saw that Karen was sitting at her desk. She had a cigarette hanging out of her mouth, her hair pulled back into a ponytail, and a small derringer handgun in right hand. She held it up and pointed it at Darla who stopped dead in her tracks. "So, are you just going to shoot me without giving me a chance to even say anything?" Darla asked. Karen smiled, but still kept the gun pointing at her. "No." she said, nonchalantly, "I will give you a chance to explain before I shoot you, but first of all, you are going to tell me where Harold is." Darla suddenly had a confused look on her face, wasn't he home, she thought. "I have no idea." Darla answered. Karen shook her head, "I know that you two have been sneaking around my back for some time, but when he didn't come home tonight, I got to thinking. Where would he go? The only answer I could find was you. So, tell me, do you have him stashed at your house or maybe your car?" Darla thought about this for a moment, she remembered Harold telling her that he had an appointment with his lawyer that afternoon after the meeting he had with the person who had called him and wanted him to meet in the wood shop. Karen shook the gun at her, "Well, I am waiting, and just saying, my patience is wearing thin." Darla put her hand up, "I don't know where he is, I assumed he was home." Karen smiled, "Well you should never assume anything Darla, when you do, it makes an ass out of you and me, now stop the bullshit and tell me where my husband is." Darla stepped forward, "Okay, just listen. He left here just before noon, he had to meet with someone back in the wood shop. He told me he would not be back the rest of the day as he had an appointment with his lawyer." Karen stood up and walked around the desk, keeping her gun trained on Darla. "Well, that is interesting Darla, but for some reason, I just do not believe you." Darla stepped back, her mouth was dry, and she could feel tiny beads of sweat forming on her forehead. "I am telling you the truth; I really have not seen him since this afternoon." Karen stopped about five feet from her, she could see that this tactic was not working. She aimed her gun at a lamp that sat on a side table next to a row of chairs that were up against the far wall. She pulled the trigger and the lamp shattered, glass falling to the floor. Darla screamed and began to head towards the door when Karen focused the gun on her again. "Stop right there you flat chested hussy, next time I pull the trigger, it is going to be at you. Now I am done playing, you tell me where my husband is, or else." Darla felt a lump in her chest, tears forming in her eyes, she did not want to die like this. She held her breath to try and stop herself from hyperventilating, but it did not seem to work. "Please." she said, but Karen did not seem to care. "Listen bitch, just tell me where he is and I will leave you alone." Darla shook her head, "I really don't know, I swear, he left here just before noon, he had a phone call from that kid he suspended on Monday. He wanted him to meet him at the wood shop in the back. He told me that he would not be back. I promise, why would I lie to you, you have a gun." Karen thought about it for a moment, she began to lower her gun, Darla felt a sigh of relief, when

Karen raised her gun again. "Take me to his office." Darla shook her head, "Okay." Karen made her go first, following her closely, keeping her gun aimed right at her back. When they reached his office door, Darla opened it slowly and turned on the light. Karen rushed past her and went to his desk. She opened the top drawer and noticed that his gun was missing. She looked up at Darla, "Where is his gun?" Darla remembered that he had taken it out and put it in his waistband. "Um, he took it with him this afternoon when he was going to meet that kid in the wood shop, I swear Karen." She walked back around the desk and stood in front of Darla. "You swear you have not seen him since he left?" Darla shook her head yes. "Well, that is funny, cause he never made it to the lawyers' office either. He was supposed to meet me there at two this afternoon." She put her gun into her pants pocket. Darla closed her eyes for a moment, she could feel her breath turning back to normal. "So here is what you don't know Darla. I had been planning on leaving this S.O.B. for over a year. The meeting we were going to have was so that we could sign divorce papers. When he did not show up I came here. His car was gone so I just assumed that he went to your house, but when I drove by there, I did not see it either. So the only logical thing to do was to call you and have you meet me here. If what you say is true, then he never left the wood shop, so, I want you to take me there."

Darla led the way from the main office through the school back to the woodshop. Karen was right behind her the whole way. Darla had a small set of keys that opened all of the classrooms that she carried on her at all times. Most of the rooms took the same key, so it was a small set. As they approached the wood shop, she fished the keys out of her pocket. Still feeling a bit nervous about the gunshot from earlier, she fumbled through the keys until she found the right one. As she began to slip the key in the lock, the door opened. Surprised by this, she hesitated to go in. "That is really odd." she said. Karen, who was standing to her right, looked over at her. "Wasn't it locked?"

Darla looked back at her as she put the keys back into her pocket. "No, it should have been though." They slowly stepped inside, and Darla looked for the light switch. Even though the sun had not set and there was still light outside, all of the shades had been pulled over the windows and only a little bit of sunlight was peeking through the open door. Darla felt her hands along the wall until she found the light switch. She clicked them on, but nothing happened. "Shit." she said. Karen pulled a small flashlight from her pocket and switched it on illuminating the classroom. To their right was a workbench that had two table saws and a scroll saw. On their left was another workbench that also contained two table saws and scroll saw. Beyond that were three rows of tables with chairs, obviously where the students sat during class. And behind that was a teacher's desk and a chalkboard. The two women looked at each other and then began to look around the room. Karen noticed something laying on the floor by the students' tables. She shone her flashlight from side to side as she carefully walked over to where she thought she spotted it. When she reached the spot, she let out a gasp. "Darla, come here, quick." Darla rushed to where she saw Karen bending over, picking something up off of the floor. "Look," she said, showing Darla what she found, "It's Harold's gun." She opened the chamber and noticed that one round was missing. "This has been shot recently." she said, as she looked the gun over. She looked back at Darla and noticed that was staring at something behind them. "What is it?" she asked. Darla, without saying a word, just pointed to something behind her. Karen slowly turned around and shone her flashlight on the chalkboard. She stood there frozen as she read a note that was sprawled out in red paint.

"The principal may have lost his head, stop the prom or you'll all be dead,"

Karen looked over at Darla, "What do you think that means?" Darla shook her head, she was not sure, there had been so many notes already this week. "I think we need to call the police." Darla finally said.

Karen shook her head in agreement, and they began to walk towards the door. "Could all of this be a prank?" Karen asked. Darla stopped and turned to face her, "I am not sure, but if your husband is missing, and neither one of us have seen him, and then there is this note, I believe that Detective Miller will want to know." Karen nodded, "Now let's get the hell out of here."

12

Detective Miller and Bradock entered the classroom slowly, flashlights in hand. "Do you think that Mr. Payne is dead?" Bradock asked. Miller turned to him slowly. Bradock noticed that his face looked like stone, showing no emotion whatsoever. When he spoke, his voice was dry. "As I told you before, I do not believe there has been a homicide and that this is an elaborate prank." Bradock was unconvinced of this notion. "Listen Miller, just because we do not have a corpse, does not mean we do have a homicide. We now have four people missing and this will be the third warning about the prom in the last three days." Miller turned to him sharply, "I know what you believe, but we have to stick to the facts, and the facts are that we have in no way found any evidence of homicide, we have no fingerprints, no signs of a struggle, no motive, and not one corpse. Yes, I know we have four people who are missing, and we will find them, but for right now, let's look at this logically." Bradock sighed heavily and went about looking through the classroom. He examined the right side, while Miller took the left side of the room. He carefully studied each one of the table saws that were mounted to the workbench. He looked at Miller, who was doing the same. "I believe we ought to have each of these dusted for prints," he said. Miller looked over at him and nodded. As he continued to look, he noticed that all of the saws were unplugged, except for one. "Didn't Darla say that the power had been cut off in this classroom, that was why the lights were not working?" he asked. Miller stood up from a crouching position, he had also noticed that all of the saws had been unplugged except one. "Yes, I believe she did." Miller answered. Bradock continued, "And I believe that it is standard practice to unplug the saws when not in use. This will help to prevent any mishaps from happening, am I correct?" Miller nodded. "Well, I find this strange, all of the saws on this bench are unplugged but one." he shone his flashlight on the middle table saw, "this one is plugged in." Miller answered back, "I also have one plugged in over here as well, it is the one in the middle." Bradock walked over to where Miller had been crouching and shone his flashlight on the floor. He noticed something red; it looked like a small red dot on the floor. "Look here," he said, Miller looking down where the light was being pointed. "Does this look like a drop of blood to you?" Miller examined it more closely, kneeling on one knee to get a better look. After a moment or two he looked back up at Bradock. "It does appear to be a small blood stain. It could have been left by anyone who has handled the saw blades in this class. Let's hope the instructor keeps good records when it comes to accidents here. In the meantime, I want this whole area sealed off, no one is allowed to come in or out until the crime team from the lab comes down here, I want every inch of this place covered." Bradock nodded, then shone his flashlight on the chalkboard. "Did you read the message this time?" Bradock asked. "Yes, and I do have to say, this message seems a bit more threatening. I am going to suggest that during the prom we place a guard at every entrance. I also want two officers patrolling the front and the back of this school as well. Now block this off and I will go and question the women who called this in."

When Miller entered the main office, he saw Karen sitting in one of the lobby chairs, while Darla sat behind her desk. The first thing he noticed was the broken lamp laying on the floor. "What happened here?" he asked. Darla looked over at Karen, then back at the detective. "I had an accident earlier while I was waiting for Karen. I accidentally knocked it over." Miller smiled and shook his head. "So tell me, why were the both of you here at such a late hour to begin with?" Karen sat up in her chair, her voice still shaky, she answered as best she could. "When Harold did not come home, I called Darla and asked her to meet me here, thinking she might know where he was." Miller smiled at that and then looked over at Darla. "Is that how it happened?" he asked. Darla shook her head. "Well let me tell you what I think, shall I?" The two women looked at each other, then back at Miller. "I think that you," he pointed to Karen, "found out about their affair and when your husband did not come home, you thought he might be here with her. Am I right so far?" Karen looked down at the floor, Darla followed suit. Miller shook his head and smiled, "Thought so. So when you got here, you accused her, there was a fight of sorts, and then you discovered that neither one of you had seen Harold, sound about right?" Karen shook her head sheepishly, Darla did too. Miller pulled one of the chairs away from the wall, faced it towards Karen, then sat down. Pulling his pad and pencil that he always carried from his shirt pocket, he began to ask more questions. "When was the last time you saw your husband, Mrs. Payne?" She looked up at him and sighed. "About six thirty this morning." "Ah, and when were you supposed to see him again?" She looked at him, then back down at the floor. "We were supposed to meet at two this afternoon at my lawyer's office to sign divorce papers." "He never showed up?" Miller asked. She shook her head no. Miller wrote this down, then turned to face Darla. "And when was the last time you saw him?" Darla looked over at Karen, then back at Miller. Her face was pale and all she could think of was the note that had been left on the chalkboard in the classroom. She drew a deep breath, then proceeded to tell Miller about the mysterious phone call that he got and the meeting he was supposed to have at noon in the classroom. "He was sure it was Doug Burton, but you need to know that he took his gun with him when he left." Miller took notice of this. "He had a weapon? You are telling me that he keeps a weapon on the school grounds?" Darla shook his head. "And were you there when he got this mysterious phone call?" Darla shook her head again, then added, "He really thought it was Doug, and he took the gun so he could scare him, he just wanted all of this to stop." Miller put his pad and pencil away then stood to his feet. "Is there anything else you can remember, like, did you hear the voice on the phone, did Payne say anything else, or did you see him after the meeting?" Darla thought for several moments, then shook her head no. "All right, I am going to need to come down to the station so we can get your statements, in the meantime, if either one of you hears from him you need to let me know right away." He turned to leave, then Darla stopped him. 'What about the prom?" she asked. Miller turned back towards her, "I think what we have going on here is a very elaborate prank that has been well thought out by two young men and it is a theory, only a theory, that maybe these two have kidnapped Mr. Payne to make it look more conferencing, however, with that being said, Mr. Payne wanted the prom to happen, so we will make it happen. Just know that there will be police stationed out front and back and patrolmen will be monitoring every door in the school cafeteria. We will keep everyone safe. Afterall, the students have earned it, just like Mr. Payne said." He turned and walked out of the office where Bradock was waiting outside for him. "What did you find out?" Bradock asked. He looked at Miller's face, it was one of the first times he was able to read something on his face, and it looked like satisfaction. Miller smiled, put his arm around Bradock's shoulder, and moved him away from the office door. "I want a tail put on Mrs. Payne right away. Also, I want a tap on her phone line and I want to know every place she has been over the past twenty-four hours." Bradock had a strange look on his face. "Wait a minute here, I am lost," he said. Miller smiled at him again. "Well, it seems that Mr. Payne was giving the business to his secretary, and Mrs. Payne found out. Now that gives her a motive, and the fact that she was trying to shoot Darla in there, I would not be one bit surprised if that blood stain in the classroom is an exact match to Mr. Payne, and ballistics will find that a bullet from Mrs. Payne's gun will match the one we find in the office here, and the one that killed her husband." Bradock looked even more puzzled. "This all sounds circumstantial." "If detective work has taught me one thing, it is to rule out every obvious circumstance and point your finger towards the more logical explanation. That is why I am not going to book her right now, but I want her followed. Also, I want every inch of this office combed. There was a broken lamp in there and I am sure it was no accident." Bradock thought for a moment, then he had another thought. "Why were they in the wood shop in the first place?" Miller smiled again, "Payne got a phone call before noon asking him to meet someone there. He never returned, then around eight tonight, Mrs. Payne called Darla to meet her here, how convenient that they just happened to go into that classroom. Now I am also sure that if you look at the writing on that chalkboard and compare it to what we had on the sidewalk here, they will not match. I think Mrs. Payne used this prank that was going on as a way to eliminate her husband and his special friend. But like you said, we have very little evidence to prove that, so let's dig around a little and see what we can find out."

Karen looked over at Darla and noticed she looked like she was in shock. "Do you think he is dead?" Darla asked. Karen smiled slightly, then stood to her feet. "I really hope so. I know, that sounds pretty petty, but at this point, I really don't care." Darla looked up at her, fear in her eyes. "Did you kill him?" Karen laughed out loud, almost in a psychotic tone. "No, oh I want to, but to be honest with you, I don't think I could kill anyone." Darla looked down at the floor and her voice was soft, Karen had to strain to hear her. "I hope he is not dead." Karen walked over to her, put her hand on Darla's chin, and raised her face to meet her gaze. "Are you really in love with him?" Darla had tears forming in her eyes. Karen noticed a single tear drop roll down her cheek. "I suppose you are, how touching." Darla noticed a hint of sarcasm in her voice. "Too bad, he is really not a good man you know, all I wanted was to have a child with him, and what did he do? He dropped me like a hot potato and went after a young tomato. Well, I tell you what Darla, if he is not dead, you can have him." Darla looked her in the eyes, "I am sorry, I never meant to hurt anyone." Karen removed her hand then smiled down at her. "Isn't that the way it always is, we never really mean to hurt anyone." She turned and headed for the door. "Were you really going to shoot me?" Darla asked. Karen turned to face her again, "Are you kidding, like a said, I don't think I could kill anyone."

13

Sara sat in front of the large mirror that sat in her bedroom. It was one of those old-fashioned vanities that her mother had bought for her when she was still a little girl. She loved to play dress up when she was young, and this was the perfect gift for her. She would sit in front of it for hours, putting on make-up, pretending she was a fashion model, and having tea parties with her friends. She sighed, she did not have very many friends when she was younger, so it was her dolls that she sat around her table. She would dress them up and have a nice place setting for them. She would pretend that they were all fashion models, and this was one of those fancy parties after a long day of shooting pictures for a magazine. She loved to play this game, she just wished she had real friends who could have come over and play with her. She looked into the mirror, brushing her hair and humming. She thought about how much she was in love with Jerry. She smiled at this thought. She wondered what it would be to make love to him. He had asked her a few times, but she just was not ready to be with him like that. She smiled as she thought about how sweet he was, not rushing her, and letting her set the pace of their relationship. How much fun she was going to have with him during the prom. She stopped and sat her brush down on the dresser. She just remembered what was going on at the school and how they were talking about shutting the prom down. This thought made her angry. Why did this have to happen, she thought. Jerry had been no nice to Homer though and prevented Doug from hitting him. She smiled, that was commendable, she thought, and she loved him for that. He was going to be the most perfect husband. He would be like her father, she thought again. He was rugged and handsome, and he reminded her of her father in that way. She had been getting ready for school and was nearly finished, she just had to put on her shoes and head to the bus stop. She did not live very far and always left early so she could meet Jerry there before the bus came. It was her favorite time of the morning. She slipped on her shoes then stood up.

As she walked to the bedroom door, she thought about how she was not going to see Homer again that morning at the bus stop. She had missed him all week and even though this was the last week of school, she was missing him. She suddenly became angry at this thought. She had heard that Homer had been suspended for selling drugs on school grounds. She clenched her fist at this thought, she had known Homer for a long time and knew that this was something he would never do. She wanted to reach out and hit something but caught herself before she punched the wall. She knew that Doug and John were behind this, and they were going to pay for it, she thought. A devious smile ran across her face at this thought. She mulled this thought over in her mind, how delicious it would be if something bad happened to them, she thought.

As she approached the bus stop, she could see Jerry standing there. Her smile disappeared to a frown as she noticed that he was talking to another girl. How could he do that, she thought, she was the only girl for him, why would he be talking to another girl? Jerry looked up and saw her and smiled. His smile melted her heart, but she could not understand why he was talking to this other girl. "Morning Sara," he said, "This is Sheila, Doug's girlfriend. She was just asking me if I had seen Doug." Sara put her arms around him in an embrace as she glanced over at Sheila as if to say, back off, he is mine. Sheila smiled faintly, "Have you seen Doug?" she asked. Sara shook her head no, then she mashed her face into Jerry's, kissing him like it was the first time she ever kissed anyone. Sheila, all of sudden, felt very uncomfortable and backed away. Jerry felt surprised ash Sara kissed him. He gently pushed her away and smiled at her. "Wow, what was that for?" he asked, his voice bewildered. Sara smiled at him, "I missed you." she said. Jerry looked back over at Sheila, "I am sorry, I have not seen him or heard from him since Monday. Have you checked with John?' Sheila shook her head, "I saw John on Tuesday, but when I went to his house last night, his mother told me he ran off and she has not seen him since he went to school Tuesday." Jerry turned to Sara, "See, I told you, something is screwy here. Doug, Homer, and John are all missing." Sheila spoke up again, "That's not all, Mrs. Hollingsworth is missing too. All of her classes have been canceled for the rest of the week. I have her for sixth period and our class was going to be making cupcakes for the prom, but her classes were canceled, and we are doing her classes with Mrs. Hibbert, the other cooking teacher." Jerry smiled, "You know, John has a huge crush on her, everyone knows it, maybe they ran off together." Sara frowned at this, "There is no way that she would ever run off with a student, especially someone as stupid as John." "Well maybe so," Jerry said, "but I still think it has something to do with Homer. I bet he is the one leaving those notes at the school, and I think he has something to do with John and Doug disappearing." Sara shook her head, "There is no way, Homer would never do anything like that." Jerry smiled at her, in the back of his mind he could not understand why she would defend him, like she had some secret crush on him or something. "Either way Sara, you can not deny that something is wrong, all three of them are missing, and both Homer and Doug were suspended, and John is the one who brought the shaving cream on the bus. I bet he has killed them and buried them down by the river or something." Sara smiled, that would be perfect she thought, but she knew Homer would never do anything like that. "I don't think so, besides, how would he have done it?" Jerry thought about that for a moment, as he began to answer, the bus pulled up, the sound drowning out his voice, so he quietly kept his theory to himself.

Everyone but Sheila boarded the bus. She watched as the doors closed and the bus pulled away from the curb. She could see Sara and Jerry sitting together and she watched them till the bus turned onto the main street and disappeared out of sight. She turned to walk away when she saw something out of the corner of her eye. It looked like someone had been standing over by the little store where the bus stop was and when she turned to see who it was, they ducked behind the store. "Hello?" she said. She was hoping it was Doug. She began to slowly walk over to the little store. It was closed and did not open till nine am, so she knew that no one was there. It was a small neighborhood market that had been here for many years. Next to it was a small storage shed and a locked walk-in outdoor freezer. There was a house that sat to the right of that, and behind the store was a small alley that led all the way down to the next street. On one side of the store side of the alley was a tall six-foot fence that stretched from behind the store to the street on both sides. On the other side of the alley was another six-foot fence that was blocked by trees and shrubs. She noticed that the alley itself was secluded from oncoming traffic and from the houses and the store on both sides. As she walked between the little store and the shed, she kept an eye out for whoever had been there just moments before. "Hello? Doug is that you?" there was no answer. There was nothing but silence and she thought maybe she had just imagined that someone was there. She felt certain though that someone had been watching them from this side of the store and she was determined to find out who it was. As she walked along, she thought she heard something behind her. She turned to look, and there was nothing. She continued to walk towards the back, calling out, but there was still no answer. She stopped, shrugging her shoulders she decided that maybe it was the owner of the store and that maybe he went into the shed. Giving up she turned to leave, and she saw someone standing there. She recognized who it was. She smiled and started to open her mouth to say hello when her face was met with a hand wearing a black glove. The gloved hand clasped around her throat. There was a confused look on her face when she looked down and saw the large gleaming knife in the other hand as it made its way from the person's side to her stomach. She blinked in confusion as she felt the pain rush to her head.

Darla sat behind Harold's desk contemplating where he could have gone or if his wife might have shot him. She seemed to be a little off of her hinges the night before. Why did she insist on going to the classroom, unless she was the one who left the message on the blackboard? She probably knew about the messages on the sidewalk because Harold had most likely told her. If she did murder him, how long would it be before she would come after her. Darla kept thinking about how Karen had shot the lamp when she did not tell her where Harold was. But then why didn't she just shoot her when they got to the wood shop, she thought. She had been puzzling over that one all night. Then she had another thought. What if she found out about the notes left on the sidewalk, the threats about the prom, decided to kill her husband, dispose of the body, and leave another note so the whole thing could be blamed on whoever left the notes in the first place. She was deep in this thought when the phone rang. She nearly jumped out of the chair. Startled, she picked up the phone and said hello. "I know you are alone." the voice said on the other end. Darla panicked. "What do you mean?" she said. There was a horrible silence on the other end of the line. It sounded like a man's voice to her, but people can disguise their voice, she thought. "Karen, I know it is you, and I know you killed your husband." she said just as bravely as she could. There was a laugh on the other end, it was almost unearthly, she thought. She felt a lump in her throat, her stomach suddenly tied in knots. "Oh, you think you are so clever?" the voice said, "and do you think the police have any idea?" Darla shuddered, the voice was creepy, dark, and foreboding, and she did not recognize it at all. "If you do not cancel the prom tomorrow night, then hell will pay you a visit." There was a click and the phone went dead. She slammed the receiver down onto the cradle and moved the chair away from the desk. She sat there for a moment not sure what to do. Maybe she could cancel the prom, it was less than twenty-four hours away and yes the students would be disappointed, but what would she rather have, the students disappointed or more people disappear? She pondered over this thought for a moment, then it was like her brain suddenly snapped back into reality. It had to be

Karen, she thought. She scooted back closer to the desk and picked up the phone. She dialed a number and listened as the phone rang on the other end. It only rang a few times before someone answered it. "Sotterville Police Department, how may I direct your call?" The voice sounded female and friendly. "I need to speak with detective Miller please." she said. "Hold one moment please." The phone went silent for a few moments, then it was answered by a familiar voice. "Miller here, give it to me." Darla sat there for a moment, then answered him. "Hello, Detective Miller, this is Darla from the high school. I wanted to tell you about a strange call I just received." "Go on." Miller said. "First of all, I believe that Karen killed her husband and now I think she wants to kill me." "Interesting." Miller said, "What did she say in the phone call?" Darla sat there a moment longer before she answered, "she said, but listen, it sounded like a man, a kind of dark brown voice if you know what I mean, like maybe a woman disguising herself as a man. She said that if the prom was still going to happen, then there would be more bad things happening. Listen though, I have a thought about this, I think she sat the whole thing up as a ruse to murder her husband and then try to pin it on a student, like I think she came up with all of these messages." Miller sat there for a moment. "Why do you think this?" he asked. Darla thought he must be putting her on, "She had a gun, she shot the lamp, she made me take her to the wood shop, and Harold got a call that morning asking him to meet someone in the wood shop. She had to have known about us and now she is going to kill me." Panic had set her voice and Miller could hear it. "Okay, listen carefully. I want you to come down to the station and meet me here and we will talk about it. We can put you in protective custody, does that sound okay to you?" Darla sat there for a moment, her heart was racing, and she knew she needed help. "Yes, give me an hour and I will be down there. You can protect me?" There was a silence on the other end of the phone for a moment, then he said, "Yes, we will make it where she can not find you." Darla sighed with relief as she hung up the phone. She really felt that if the police would really protect her, she would be okay. She stood up from behind the desk and made her way towards the door when the phone rang again. She paused for a moment and thought about whether she should answer it or not. It continued to ring, she felt maybe she should answer it and walked back over to the desk. When she picked up the receiver and said hello, there was a dial tone. Whoever had been calling had already hung up before she answered it. She sat the receiver back on the cradle and walked out of the office.

When she reached the outer office, she sat down at her desk and began going through the notes and paperwork that was laying there. As she was going through them, she saw one about Mrs. Hollinsworth, she had been out sick or something since Tuesday. She shrugged this off, she knew her classes were being covered by a substitute. Then she saw something she had not seen before. There was a little envelope, like one of those kinds that were like a thank you card would be in. It had her name on it. As she picked it, she looked around to see if anyone was still there that could have put it on her desk. She did not see anyone, but she looked again just to double check. She turned it over and saw that it was sealed. She reached into her desk drawer and pulled out an envelope opener. It looked like a small dagger in her hand. She worked quickly to open it. As she pulled out the card, she noticed that it simply said Harold on the front. She smiled, maybe he wasn't dead after all and he had sent her a note to let her know that he was okay. She opened the card, her face turned three shades of blue. On the inside of the card was a lock of bloody hair. She tried to scream, but the scream was stuck in her throat. She threw the card on the desk and stood up as quickly as she could. She backed away from the desk, still trying to scream, but she felt stifled and nothing but a small gasp came out of her mouth. She scrambled for the front door and as she went outside, she looked around. There was no one there. She ran as fast as she could towards her car. When she reached her destination, she realized that she had left her keys in her desk drawer. Panicked, she did not want to go back to her desk. She frantically looked around to see if anyone else was in the parking lot. It was completely empty. She looked back towards the office. What if the person who had placed the card on her desk was still hiding in there, she thought? She looked down at the pavement, then back to the office. It was a risk she was willing to take. She began to walk briskly back to the office, keeping her surroundings in total view. She looked over towards the library. Maybe Mrs. Fredricks could just give her ride to the police station, she thought. She realized that if anything was going to be done about this, she would need the note to give to Detective Miller. She concentrated on getting back to the office, getting her keys, the note, then she would go to the police station. As she opened the door to the office she looked around. Everything still looked the way it did when she had bolted out. She quickly walked over to her desk and opened her desk drawer where she always kept her car keys. They were not there. She felt her heart leap into her throat. She had remembered putting them there when she arrived that morning. She backed up from her desk then she noticed that the card was not where she had laid it. Now she was really panicking. Her breathing had turned heavy, and she could feel her heart thumping in her chest. There was a sound like a door clicking shut. She looked towards Harold's door and realized the sound had come from there. She put her hand on her chest hoping that would stop her heart from pounding. She slowly walked around to the door that led to the principal's office. She reached out for the doorknob and grasped it. As she began to turn it slowly, she stopped. What if it was Karen, she thought? This could be a trap and then Karen would kill her too. She removed her hand from the door and began to back away when she bumped into something. She stopped, she felt like her heart would quit beating any moment, and it felt like her stomach just fell to the floor. She wanted to turn around, but she felt frozen to where she was standing. Suddenly there was a hand wearing a black glove in front of her and she saw as it clasped over her mouth. She tried to scream again, but this time it was muffled by the hand. She tried to run, but she could not. Suddenly, there was another hand clad in a black glove in front of her and it was holding her letter opener. Her eyes widened and she tried to shake her head no as the hand plunged it deep into her neck.

14

The sun began to set over Sotterville as Bradock made his way through the city streets. His mind wandered over the last four days. He had looked at all the evidence trying to piece the puzzle together, but nothing made sense. He had no leads, he had no corpse, not one single shred of evidence to connect the three missing boys, and now the principal too. He was heading back to the police station after going over all of the crime scenes again, he felt that something just did not add up. He muddled through all the events that had taken place since Monday. The two males, Homer and Doug, had been in a fight. Doug was suspended that morning. A phone call came into the office with someone reporting that Homer had been selling drugs. He was then suspended. Bradock stopped with his thought process for a moment. There had to be a connection there. The person who made the call to the high school, maybe it was the second person who was missing, maybe it was John. His mother had stated that he and Doug were friends. What if Doug had convinced John to make the call for him? Bradock thought for a moment, this could be a possibility, Doug's way of getting some kind of revenge. With both of them missing, and within twenty-four hours of each other, it could make sense that they could be in hiding till everything blew over. He thought back about what Miller had told him about Homer, that he was in protective custody. This did not make any sense to him, and even if Homer was, it would be a breach for the family to say so. He had done some further investigation about this and came up with nothing. He wanted to talk to Miller about it again, but he had been busy. When he pulled into the police station parking lot he noticed that Miller's car was still there. He parked his car and continued to think about everything else. The blood mixed into the paint, the strange messages on the sidewalk, this disappearance of Mr. Payne, was this all an elaborate prank? He stepped out of his car and began to walk to the entrance of the station when he noticed someone standing on the side of the building. He paused for a moment to see who it was, but he could not make them out. The person stood about five feet eight inches, and they were dressed all in black. He squinted his eyes, but with the sun setting, it cast dark shadows across the person's face, and he could not tell who it was. "You, who are you, and what are you doing over there?" There was no answer. He noticed a strange stillness in the air and the hairs on the back of his neck stood up. He felt a cold chill go down his spine. He watched as the person slowly backed up, turning their back to him, they began to go around to the back side of the building. Bradock thought for a moment, he did not know who it was and was not sure he should pursue them. He had a strange feeling that he just could not shake off, like maybe this was one of the teenagers who had disappeared. Before they completely moved out of sight, Bradock called to them again. "Wait, don't go, I can help you." There was still no reply. There was no time to waste, he thought, and he began to go after them. In the back of his mind he heard his inner voice tell him not to take any chances, so he drew his side arm. He had never had to pull out his pistol before and he usually only kept one round in the chamber. He had never really had the need for it but thought that one bullet would be all he would ever need.

He came around the back of the building, his pistol in the ready position, just in case. He could not see anyone. The back of the building was like any other building. There were two back doors that led to a small parking lot where three police vehicles sat. The station itself was two stories tall. There were two yellow lights over each door and a large parking lot light that had not yet turned on. He faced the building and examined both doors. They were locked from the inside to prevent anyone from coming in the back way to try and surprise anyone. Each door had a special keypad lock on the outside and only the commissioner and the captain had the codes. If anyone was bringing a suspect in through the back, they would radio the desk sergeant who would have another officer meet them at the back and open the door from the inside. The doors looked untouched, so he turned his attention to the three police cars that were in the parking lot. The sun had completely set and it was now dark. Knowing that the light would come on at any time, he hesitated to move from where he was standing until there was more light. He turned to the other side of the building, it sat adjacent to the courthouse only separated by a few shrubs that grew in between it and the station. The parking lot light began to blink into life, illuminating the lot with its fluorescent yellow glow. Bradock, still standing in the same spot, could not see the parking lot as it stretched out before him. The three police cars were parked parallel next to each other, with only a few feet between them. Just enough space to open a door, he thought. He crouched down to peer under them, just to see if anyone would be foolish enough to hide under them, he saw nothing. That meant that there was no one under them, behind them, or in between them as he could not see anything, not even any feet. He turned his back to them and began to focus his attention on the opposite side of the building. He slowly made his way around to the side, making sure to keep his perimeter in view at all times. Feeling a little antsy, he placed his back up against the back side of the police station, then he slowly peered around the corner, holding his pistol now in both hands, his finger on the trigger, just in case. This side of the station had no lights. There were five shrubs in all that separated the station from the courthouse, and they stood about five feet tall. First, he checked for any movement. There did not appear to be any, but a person could hide in the shrubs easily if they wanted to. He stepped around the corner cautiously, keeping his eyes open and watching the shrubs. He still did not see anything. As he approached the first plant, he ran his hand through it and did not feel anything. He began to feel silly, whoever had been standing there could have been anyone. He smiled and shook his head. "This case is getting to you old man." he said out loud. He removed his hand from the shrub and turned to go to the back of the building. As he began to step away, someone stepped out from behind the second shrub. They had on black gloves and were holding a huge rock. As Bradock began to walk back to the parking lot, they swiftly moved up behind him, staying as silent as they could. The rock came crashing down onto Bradock's head and he made a grunting sound as he fell to the ground. Then slowly, the black gloved hands drug him into the darkness.

Miller sat at his desk looking over the file for Mr. Payne. He closed the file, stood to his feet, and walked to the office door. He spied the desk sergeant behind the counter and called out to him. "Any word from Bradock yet?" he asked. The sergeant looked up from the crossword puzzle he was working on and shook his head no. Miller smiled, "Thank you, if you hear anything from him, please let me know." He shut his office door then walked back over to his desk. He fumbled through a small stack of papers until he found what he was looking for. It was a small piece of paper with a number scribbled on it. He picked up the receiver from his phone and dialed the number. It rang three times, then someone answered. "Hello." the voice on the other end of the phone said. "Miller here. How is it going down there?" The voice hesitated for a moment, then answered. "There has not been any movement since about noon today. Mrs. Payne came out and checked her mail, then went back inside. She has not gone anywhere, and she has not had any visitors. Are you sure about this Miller?" Miller sighed, "Yes I am sure, I believe she killed her husband and I believe she is going to go after Darla, that cute secretary her husband was having an affair with. Now you just sit tight and keep an eye on her and if she moves, you follow, you got that?" "Listen Miller, I don't think the chief is going to like us hanging around down here when she is not going anywhere and doing this on your hunch could get us all in hot water." Miller sighed again, "You just let me handle the chief, my gut says she did it and any minute she is going to go after that secretary, now just sit tight." He hung up the phone and snorted, snot nosed kids, he thought. He had been doing this a lot longer than they had and if he had a hunch, it was usually right. He picked up his hat from his desk and put it on top of his head. Where the hell was Bradock, he thought, he should have been back here by now. He walked over to the door. He looked at his watch, it was ten thirty. The day had gotten away from him and Darla never did come down to the police station. He had waited for her all day, but she never showed up. He sighed again. He should have sent a car to pick her up, she had sounded so panicked. But when she never came, he felt that she might be okay, and with Karen Payne not leaving her house, she would be safe. "Miller." the desk sergeant said, "That woman from the high school never came down here today, you want I should call her house." "No need, I am going down to the school now." The desk sergeant looked at his watch, "Yeah, no sense waiting till the last minute. It's like ten thirty, you really think anyone is going to be at the high school at this hour?" Miller smiled, "Yeah you are right, maybe I should go to her house, do you have that address handy?" He shuffled through some papers sitting on his desk till he came across her report from the night before. "Yeah, got it right here. It is 137 Walnut." Miller said thanks, then headed for the front door. When he walked outside, he noticed that Bradock's car was sitting in the parking lot. "Well that is funny." he said, then turned around and walked back inside. "That was a short trip." the desk sergeant said, halfway grinning. Miller walked up to the sergeants station, "Are you sure Bradock didn't come in here?" "No, I have not seen him since he left earlier today. Said he was going to go back over to the Burton's address and look at the shed again." "Well, his car is outside." Miller looked around then looked back at the sergeant, "Okay, get a flashlight, you are going to help me look outside, then I want this building searched from top to bottom, I want Bradock found, is that understood?" Miller's face had gone from calm to unreadable and the desk sergeant knew this meant business. He pulled out a large flashlight from inside the desk and came around to the front. He stood about six feet five inches, just two inches taller than Miller. "Okay, I want you to check the back parking lot and side by the courthouse, I am going to check the front parking lot and the other side of the building, meet me back by the front door in five minutes, unless you see something, then you holler, got it?" He nodded and the two of them walked out.

Miller began looking around the front parking lot, while the desk sergeant headed around the side in between the station and the courthouse. He turned on his light and shone it on the shrubs that separate the two buildings. He did not have to look very long when he noticed a body laying between two of the shrubs. He swallowed hard as he approached the body that was laying there. He turned and yelled for Miller. Turning back to the body, he bent down to get a closer look. The body was lying on their back. He knelt to get a better look. Shining his flashlight over the body, he noticed a large lump on the back of their head. The person's hair was matted with blood, and he felt certain it was Bradock. He took him by the shoulder and gently turned him over just as Miller walked up, He shone his flashlight on the person's face. "Is it Bradock?" Miller asked. "It is, but you better call for a bus, he is still alive, but his breathing is really shallow." Miller took a step back and removed the walkie talky from his belt. "This is Miller, I need a bus at the police station, officer down." He clipped it back to his belt, then looked around. "Did you see anyone?" he asked. The desk sergeant looked back up at him, "This is as far as I got, I must have scared off whoever did this, but I did not see anyone." Miller put his hand on his shoulder, "Thanks, great work. You stay here with him; I am going to look around." Miller stepped around them and continued looking, the desk sergeant took Bradock's hand. "Hang in there buddy, help is on the way." Miller probed through each of the shrubs as he walked along while keeping his eye out on Bradock and the desk sergeant. In the far distance he could hear the sound of the ambulance as it made its way to the police station. When he got to the back of the building, he saw the three cars that were parked there. He crouched down to look under them but did not see anything. He walked over to the cars and using his flashlight, he peered into the back seats of all three vehicles. He did not see anything. He focused his attention on the two back doors, but nothing looked out of place. Satisfied that there was no one there, he made his way back over to where Bradock was lying. As he approached them, he noticed that the EMTs were there and looking Bradock over. He listened as one of the EMTs contacted the hospital, "His BP is 99 over 71 and holding, IV started, preparing for transport now to Sotterville Trauma Unit." Miller walked over as close as he could without getting in their way. "Is he going to be okay?" Miller asked. One of the EMTs looked up at him, "He is going to be okay; it looks like he sustained a fracture on the back of his head, probably with a blunt instrument, and he is going to have a serious concussion, it was a good thing you found him when you did though, ten more minutes and he would not have made it." Miller's face went blank and he lost all expression. He stood there watching them as they loaded him into the back of the ambulance.

15

JERRY STOOD IN THE middle of the library study hall surveying the work he had completed. This was the largest room in the library, and it consisted of ten tables that were laid out for students to study or read. There were five large rectangular tables that normally outlined the outer part of the room. In the middle of the room were five round tables that could sit up to six people. They had moved the tables so that the round tables were at one end of the room, this is where Jerry had laid out the books that were for sale. The remaining tables were put together to make two long tables with room in between them for people to walk on both sides. This is where the Civil War memorabilia had been placed. The fifth table sat up against the wall by itself, this was where the professor from the college would be sitting so students could approach him to ask questions. Mrs. Fredricks had also sat up a small cash register at this same table for students who wanted to buy books. As he looked around, Jerry was proud of the work he had put into the display. As he looked around the room, he admired the old muskets and firearms from that time period. He was able to handle almost every piece from the collection and there were twelve in all. His favorite was an Aston Model 1842 precision pistol with a walnut stock and brass fittings that held it all together. The professor had told him that it still fired and was a fun gun to shoot. He noticed that there were about four rounds of ammunition in a small glass container that sat next to the pistol. He was standing there admiring it when Mrs. Fredricks tapped him on the shoulder. He jumped just a little and turned to face her. "Oh, it's only you." he said, his face starting to flush. She smiled at him, "Really cool stuff huh?" He smiled back. He had felt like she had been the librarian there at the school since the dawn of time, however; he enjoyed working for her and she never gave him any trouble. "It is really cool," he picked up the pistol, "I would love to have a crack at shooting this sucker." She smiled again and then motioned for him to sit back on the table. "Well Jerry, they are looking, not touching. Are you going to the prom tonight?" Jerry placed the pistol back in its spot then turned to face her again. "Yes, I will be picking up Sara around seven since the prom doesn't start till eight." His smile began to disappear and was replaced by a small frown. "I am actually surprised that Mr. Payne did not cancel the prom after all those stupid threats, and then with John and Doug missing, it just does not feel right." She looked over at all the tables, then looked at the clock on the wall, it was only ten after eight in the morning, the bell would be ringing for first period soon, and she had not sold any books yet or had anyone come in to look at the display. She looked back at Jerry, "I know and with Mr. Payne out the rest of the week too." Jerry looked at her sharply, his eyes widened, and his face went pale. "Mr. Payne is out?" She shook her head yes, "I think he has some kind of flu; Mrs. Hollingsworth has been out all week too." Jerry shuddered at this news. "That seems kind of strange doesn't it, I mean after all of the weird things that have been going on this week." She shrugged her shoulders. She could care less, she thought. Today was the last day of school and graduation being next week. She was going to go on a permanent vacation as she was going to retire this year. She had not really told anyone about it and could not care less. There were too many rumors that circulated this place, and the more she kept to herself, the better. "Son, there are always weird things going on in this place. After four years, haven't you noticed that?" She smiled at him again, then turned and walked away. Jerry felt his stomach churn. This could not be a coincidence, there had to be some kind of connection, he thought. He closed his eyes and thought as hard as he could. Doug and John were both missing and so was Homer. He thought back to what had happened on the bus Monday morning. They had played a horrible trick on Homer that turned into a fight. He knew Homer had been picked on before and even though he stood up for him, he could have been a better friend. He had heard that both Homer and

Doug were suspended, meaning that neither of them could go to the prom. He suddenly had a terrible revelation. What if they were not just missing, he thought, what if they were dead? What if they had been murdered and no one had found their bodies? He tried to shake off this thought, he could not believe that Homer could be violent or even kill anyone. He could not shake the feeling that something bad had happened to them. He had known Doug and John almost all of his life and they had never ran off before. It was not something Doug would do. John, maybe, but Doug was the kind of person that did not run away from anything. Then he had another thought, what if Doug had framed Homer with the drugs? Everyone in school knew that Homer was a square and that he would never do anything like that. Maybe this triggered something inside of him, he thought, if that was the case, then he could have snapped, but where would he have hidden the bodies? He was contemplating this thought when he heard the bell ring. He walked over a large window that faced the street. As he looked out of the window, he began to formulate a plan. He could ditch out of the library, that was no problem, then he could go search for them. Maybe he could find them and maybe they would be okay. He could search Homer's house and see if maybe he had taken them there. Maybe they were tied up in his basement. Yeah, Homer was not a very strong person, but what if he took them by surprise and overpowered them. He shook his head; he knew he was not that brave or that strong and Homer would not even be smart enough to come up with an idea like that. He looked down at the floor, the light gone from his eyes. He did not know where Homer lived. He stood there thinking for a moment, then his eyes lit up again. Sara would know, he thought. He looked around to see if Mrs. Fredricks was watching him. He could not see her. In the study hall of the library was a side door that led out towards the principal's office, if he could sneak out that door, then he could make his way across the campus to the girl's gym, this is where Sara was during first period. If he could get there without being caught, maybe he could convince her to tell him where Homer lived. Maybe, he thought, he could even convince her to take him there. A smile began to creep across his face as he made his way to the side door.

He slowly cracked the door open and peered outside. He checked both sides of the door, then looked back into the library to make sure he was not being watched. He did not see anyone, so he opened the door wider and slipped out. Closing the door softly behind him, he looked again to make sure that no one was watching. He shut the door and began to make his way into the school grounds. The girl's gym lay on the other side of the campus and would take a couple of minutes to get there. He thought that he could go out to the street and take the sidewalk around, this would take longer, but it could cut the risk of him being seen through any open classroom windows. He rethought this; it would be much faster if he just cut through the school. He could go around the office and behind the auditorium to the gym, this would prevent him from going in front of any of the classrooms and he could duck into the restrooms on the other side of the office he was spotted. It was times like this that he wished he still had his phony hall pass he had made when he was a freshman. He made his way stealthily through the school, avoiding any open windows, and only having to duck between buildings once or twice when he saw a maintenance man. He ducked back behind the large school auditorium that lay between the office and side street. He could see the sign for the Dairy Freeze on the other side and for a moment he thought he could cross the street and just make a phone call to get Sara out of school. He brushed that thought aside as the more he thought about it, the more stupid it sounded. From where he stood, he could also see the girls gym, now if only he can get to her without the coach seeing him. The gym was a large building that was attached to the girl's locker room that lay on the far side. Inside, it was in reality, a basketball court with rows of seating on either side. There were two doors that lead into the gym. One on the side he was standing, this door was never open and was always locked. On the other side of the gym were two doors. There was a field next to the gym and in front of the gym where the two doors were another basketball court and beyond that was a tennis court. Hoping that the class was being held in the gym, he began to move to the side of the building and start towards the front doors. He heard the sound of laughter and stopped. The class was being held outside and he saw Sara standing next to one of the basketball hoops. Trying to be as inconspicuous as possible, he tried to get her attention by waving at her. It seemed this tactic was working as he noticed that she looked over and saw him. She let out a giggle at the sight of him backed up against the side of the gym waving to her. She looked over to see if the coach was looking, her back was turned to the class, so she saw her opportunity to run over to him. She kissed him on the cheek then smiled. "What are you doing here?" she asked. He looked at her, she had such perfect eyes, he thought. The way she smiled melted his heart. "I have a favor to ask." She put her hands on his hips and smiled again. "Sure, what do you need?" He put his hands over hers. She noticed the smile disappeared from his face and he looked as if he just swallowed a lemon. "Do you know where Homer lives?" he asked. She moved her hands from his hips and stepped back. The smile gone from her face; her eyes widened in surprise. "Why?" she asked. He blinked then looked to his left and to the right, leaning into her ear, he whispered, "I think he has either killed or kidnapped Doug and John." A look of disgust came on her face, and she shrugged her shoulders. "First of all, how could you think such a stupid think, and second of all, even if I did know where he lived, why in the hell would I tell you after a stupid comment like that. You are no better than everyone else around here." She backed away from him again. He had a look of disappointment on his face as he tried to move closer to her again. "I am so sorry, I know it sounds crazy because I just don't see Homer being that vindictive or even violent, it was just a hunch. I will just forget about it." She smiled, "I know, it seems really crazy with Doug and John missing, but I am sure there is a good explanation for it all, and when we find out what it is, we all have a good laugh out of it." Jerry smiled and gave her a hug, but in the back of his mind he just could not shake off this feeling.

16

Bradock slowly opened his eyes. He could smell the faint odor of disinfectant mixed with urine. In the background he could hear the hum of a machine and what he thought sounded like a heart monitor. His head felt like it was going to explode, his mouth tasted like a pickle. At first, he could not see, it was like opening his eyes and looking directly into the sun. He squinted but this did not help. He closed his eyes again, then raised his hands to rub them. He noticed that his right arm was constricted, and he could not move it very well. "Well, look at you, waking up and all," He recognized the voice. He tried to talk, but his throat was dry, and it came out only as a whisper. "Where am I?" he asked. The voice came to him again, only this time a little closer. "You are in the ICU unit in the hospital. Seems like someone thought they would go and hit you on the head with a rock." Bradock smiled faintly, still trying to get used to the light, he opened his eyes again. He could see a little, but everything seemed a bit fuzzy. He groaned a little as he moved his left hand over his face and head. He could feel the bandages on his head and wondered how all of this happened. He could make out a person standing beside the hospital bed. Miller reached out and put his hand on Braddock's arm. "I understand it was lucky I found you, a few more minutes and you have been a goner." Bradock smiled faintly, he had to stop, if felt like his face was going to break. "What happened?' he asked in a voice that was barely audible. Miller took a small step closer to the bed so he could whisper into Braddock's ear. "I was hoping you could tell me. I had been waiting for you at the station and when you didn't show, I decided I was going to leave. I saw your car in the parking lot and, well, went looking for you. I found you on the side of the building between the station house and the courthouse. The EMTs said you had been hit on the back of the head with something, so we did some searching after they brought you here. We found a rock the size of Gibraltar laying five feet away from where you were found." He leaned even closer into his ear, looked around to make sure no one was listening, then continued to talk to him. "The rock we found had skin and bone fragments that matched yours, but we could not find any fingerprints on it. Whoever hit you over the head must have been wearing gloves at the time." Bradock had a pained look on his face, and when he tried to speak, nothing came out. Miller patted him on the arm and smiled down at him. "Don't worry, we will catch the son of a bitch that did this, you just try and get some rest and feel better." He started to turn, then turned back to face Bradock, "Oh, we caught Mrs. Payne, we brought her into the station this morning, you know, just to talk with her, and she confessed to the whole thing. She said that she had made up the whole scheme with the notes at the school and was going to frame that Doug boy her husband had suspended. Her plan was to kill him and Darla for having an affair. She is in central booking now." Bradock smiled faintly at him, then closed his eyes and drifted off to sleep. Miller looked at his watch, it read two thirty. "I need to get going, you get better, and I will keep you updated." Even though Bradock's eyes were closed, he waved to him as he left the room. Bradock lay there, his head felt like a ton of bricks had fallen on it, but in the back of his mind this did not seem right. He was puzzled over how Doug Burton's blood was mixed into the paint that was used on the sidewalk. He heard the door click shut as Miller exited the room then he tried to relax.

Miller stood in the lobby of the ICU. He noticed a nurse sitting behind one of the stations and approached her. "Good afternoon," he said, "I am Detective Miller and that patient in room two is my partner. I am going to be sending a policeman up here to keep an eye on him. Someone tried to kill him last night, and I think that person might be back." The nurse shuddered, "have you talked to security?" she asked. Miller shook his head no, "I do not want to get others involved. I think his life is still in danger and I want around the clock police protection while he is here, I also do not want him getting the idea that he needs to leave." The nurse picked up the phone, "I am going to call the doctor in charge." She dialed a number and placed the receiver to ear. Miller could hear the phone ringing from where he stood. "Hello, Doctor Franks, I have a Detective Miller here, his partner is the one in room two. He is sending a policeman up here to watch over him. He believes that his life may still be in danger." She was silent for a moment while the Doctor talked to her, "Okay, I will let him know." She hung the phone up, "He said that would be fine, he will also keep an eye on him as well, but you will still need to notify security and the Chief of Medicine." Miller nodded, "Okay, I will take care of that, he is a good man, please do not let anything happen to him." She smiled at him, then he turned to leave. As he got into his car, he reached for his police radio and opened the mike. "Headquarters, this is Miller, I am just now leaving Bradock. I want an officer here at once posted outside his door, I want a change of guard every six hours, over." He let go of the button on the mike, the radio hissed for a moment, then he was met with a response. "Roger, Headquarters here, desk sergeant Hatch, sending Officer Moony out to the hospital, will have Officer Sexton relieve him in six hours, over and out" Miller smiled as he put the mike back in place, started his car, and drove away.

At the high school, the cafeteria buzzed with activity as the student committee began decorating for the night's big event. There was a fresh linen tablecloth on every table. A place was set or every couple that would be there. A table was set up with a large punch full and cups for refreshments. Next to the were the cupcakes the cooking class had made earlier in the week. A disco ball hung in the center of the room while the stage was set up for a live band. A section in the middle of the room was made clear so a dance floor could be set up. Tinsel and streamers were being hung from the ceiling while a banner was being hung by the stage. The banner was at least nine feet long and read, "Dreams come true in 84" in bright red and gold letters. Red and gold were the school's colors, and the banner had the graduating class motto. A special table had been set aside for this year's prom king and queen while a corkboard that hung on the wall behind it held pictures of previous years king and queens all the way back to 1956. The back doors of the cafeteria swung open, and the band began to pour through the doors bringing in their equipment. As they set up their instruments on stage, the maintenance man ducked behind the stage to a door that led to the room where the electrical equipment was placed. It was a small room, five by five and held all the switches and breakers for the cafeteria. The switches were for the special lights that had been installed for the stage. There was a small table at the back of the room where the control panel for the sound system and lighting sat. All of the night's magic would happen right here on this panel. He sat down in the chair that faced the table and began completing sound checks for the band. He also tested every light to make sure they were all in working order. This was his favorite thing to do, he had been the maintenance man for almost fifteen years and when they installed this magnificent electrical piece of art, he had been the man behind the controls ever since. He felt a sense of pride as he used this control panel, like he was the personal magician behind the magic and the real master of the show. One of the band members stepped into the room and gave him a thumbs up. "Hey Ed, it sounds great out here, we might need just a little more bass." Ed smiled and turned back to the master control and audio mixer sitting before him. He found the knob labeled bass and turned all the way to the right till it reached the number ten. Everything was going to be perfect, he thought.

17

Jerry did not have a car, but he had his driver's license. This was the one time his father would let him borrow his 1979 Mustang. He loved this car and was never allowed to drive it. He was heading to pick up Sara for the prom. He was dressed in a black tux with a white ruffled buttoned-down shirt. Of course, his mother said he looked handsome, but what did mother's know, he thought. As long as Sara liked how he looked, he did not care. He thought it was strange that she asked him to pick her up at the bus stop. When he got there, she was waiting for him. He thought she looked dazzling in her pink dress. It was form fitting and was cut just a half an inch above the knee. Her hair was curled and feathered back, the shoulders of her dress were ruffled just a bit, not over done like other prom dresses he had seen. It was not cut too low in front, but just enough so he could make out her cleavage. He smiled when she opened the car door to get in. "Are you ready to make all your dreams come true?" he asked. She smiled at him, but never said a word as she sat in the passenger seat. He looked over and saw her knee, she caught him and pulled her dress down just enough to cover it. "Don't worry Sara, I am not going to attack you." She giggled, "And why not?" His eyes widened, his face turned a bright red, "Umm, I didn't think that was on the menu!" She giggled again. "You never know what might happen tonight." He had made reservations at The Oak Pit, a steakhouse in town, for five thirty. All through the meal, he could not take his eyes off of her. She was as radiant as he had ever seen her before. Her smooth silky skin, her beautiful eyes, her red lips, even her nose, he thought, looked better than anything that sat on the plate in front of them. He wanted her, but in the back of his mind he knew that was not going to happen, but he was okay with that. He had already promised her that he would never ask her to do anything she was not ready to do, and even on the most romantic night of his life, he would keep that promise. There were still a lot of things he did know about her, and he had never met her family. He did not know if she had any brothers or sisters, and she never spoke about her parents. Her home life was very private, but he was okay with that. On the other hand, she had never met his family either. Maybe if they stayed together and were married, that would be different, he thought. She noticed how he had been looking at her, so she smiled at him. He would make a great husband someday, she thought. She was not certain if she would ever get married, have a family, have a life outside of the life she already had. They barely spoke to each other during their meal. A few times she had slipped her foot onto his, or they held hands. Jerry finally broke the silence. He raised his glass, it was only soda pop, but he didn't care. "Here is a toast to us, that we are able to have every dance to ourselves tonight, and every dance we have from now on we have with each other." She raised her glass and they put them together. "I will drink to that," she said, "and I will add this, that tonight's endeavors will be fully fulfilled." She lifted her glass to her mouth, and with one gulp, she downed the entire contents. He took a sip of his soda, then placed his glass back on the table. What did she mean by that, he thought? He was about to ask her when she suddenly stood to her feet. "You better pay the check Jerry, that dance is going to start without us. I am going to go and powder my nose while you do that." She turned on her heels and trotted towards the bathroom. Jerry had a stunned look on his face. He reached into his back pocket and pulled out his wallet. He removed some bills and placed them on the table. As he was putting his coat back on, she emerged from the bathroom. She smiled at him, took his hand, and led him back out into the street where the car was parked.

Jerry noticed a police car sitting in the parking lot as he pulled into the high school. He was using the back parking lot that was between the cafeteria and the woodshop. He stepped out, walked over to the other side of the car then opened the door for Sara. He watched as she glided out of the passenger seat. Off in the distance he could hear the live music from inside the cafeteria. They were playing some sort of song from a popular hair band. He recognized the tune as it was one of those songs that the radio had overplayed during this school year. He thought they sounded good though for a cover band, and in the back of his mind he never thought he would go to a prom where there was a real band. "Care to join me to that most audacious party that is going on right now?" he said as he shut the door. "I sure as hell do!" she said with a smile, then they hooked arms and began to walk towards the party. As they made their way to the door, he glanced over to look at the parked police car. He remembered overhearing that they were going to have some patrol officers keeping an eye on the place due to the strange notes that had been left. He could make out the outline of what looked like an officer sitting in the driver's side of the car. He smiled at them, but he could not tell if they smiled back. Then they disappeared through the doors of the cafeteria. Inside the police car, the officer sat at the wheel. His hands were to his side, his eyes wide open, and blood was pouring from his neck.

Jerry opened the door for Sara. His ears were hit with a blast of rock and roll music. As he entered the cafeteria it was like entering into a whole new world. The disco ball was turning, casting glittering light over the whole room. Above the stage blue, red, and green lights flashed giving the whole room an unearthly glow that continued to flash. The lights reflecting off of the tinsel and streamers that hung over the people that were dancing feverishly to the loud rhythms of the live band. The lead singer, dressed in ripped blue jeans and white tux jacket, danced around the stage as he belted out a familiar tune. He and Sara were met by a bubbly blond girl, he recognized her as one of the senior cheerleaders. "Jerry and Sara, "she said in her bubbly voice, "here are your name tags, make sure to cast your ballot for king and queen." She pointed to the right, "Refreshments are over there," then she pointed to the tables that surrounded the dance floor, "you can sit at any of the tables. Have fun you two!" She handed them the tags, smiled at them, then turned around and walked away. She was wearing a dress that was a blue metallic color. It had one puffed sleeve that seemed to hug her neck, while the other side seemed to drape over her shoulder. It was cut at least five inches above her knee. She was also wearing dark black nylons, and Jerry noticed they looked like they were made out of spider webs. As she turned, Jerry looked down and he could see her panty line, and as she walked away, Jerry noticed how tight the dress was around her butt. Sara saw that he was watching her walk away, and she slightly hit his arm. "Am I going to have to keep my eye on you all night long?" she asked in a giggly voice. He turned and looked at her, "No, she is not near as pretty as you." Her eyes narrowed slightly and a devilishly grin crawled onto her face. "Pretty huh, well it was not her face you were looking at." She took his hand and led him to the dance floor, "Just keep your eyes on me while we dance the night away." He smiled at her as he took her in his arms, and they began to dance. From behind the stage, a person peered into the crowded room. Their eyes watched everyone as they danced and mingled through the party. When they saw Jerry and Sara twirling on the dance floor, their eyes narrowed with hate.

Ed sat at the controls in the room behind the stage. He was having the time of his life working the control panel. His wife had just bought him a Walkman and he was wearing his headphones. Even though he enjoyed working the audio mixer, he did not particularly care for this kind of music. He really preferred a good country song and his wife and made him a great mixed tape. He knew that even though he needed to hear the sounds that were going on through the door, he was still able to listen to his music through the headphones that connected to the small cassette player that was attached to his belt. He was almost sixty years old, and he never thought in his life he would ever see such a small player. The cassette deck he had at home was at least five sizes bigger than this. He had a really nice stereo system at home. It consisted of a turntable, cassette player, and an eight-track player. He knew that if he turned it up too loud it would shatter the windows. He was proud of his stereo. As he sat there watching the sound levels, the door behind him slowly opened. He noticed for only a moment that music coming from the other side of the wall sounded louder for a moment, but it was not enough to make him curious enough to turn around. He was bobbing his head back and forth to an old Hank Williams tune that was currently drumming into his ears, so he did not notice that a person had slipped in and was standing behind him. Suddenly his head was met with a very hard object, and he slumped over in his chair, hitting his head on the table that held the audio mixer. A hand covered with a black glove grabbed Ed by the hair and yanked him out of the chair, dumbing his body on the floor. The person did not waste any time. They pulled a lump of paper out of their pocket along with a book of matches. They placed the paper on the soft seat of the chair. The hands struck a match and put it under the little clump of paper. The fire began to burn brightly, and it flickered in their eyes. They turned and slowly slipped back out the door. The fire spread from the chair to the table in a matter of moments. Smoke began to billow out under the door, causing the lights that were flashing to appear like they were flashing through fog.

Jerry stopped dead in tracks when he noticed the smell of something burning. Sara looked at him, a confused look on her face. "Do you smell that?" he asked. She tilted her head back and sniffed the air. "It smells like something is burning." she said. Jerry looked around towards the stage and noticed the smoke that was filtering through the stage. "Maybe it is the band, I know a lot of bands that use special effects like smoke and pyrotechnics." she said. Jerry looked at it, then shook his head. "No, something doesn't seem right about it, I am going to go check it out." He gently pushed her aside and turned towards the stage. The smoke looked like it was getting thicker and no one else seemed to notice. The band was still rocking out like they owned the place, they had not noticed the smoke either. Jerry pushed his way past the other couples that were dancing till he reached the side of the stage. By this time, he had to cover his mouth as it seemed the smoke was growing much thicker. He walked behind the stage and noticed that the smoke was coming from behind the closed door. He walked over towards the door just as the music died out. He looked up and noticed that the lights began to flicker as the room was plunged into total darkness except for the flickering of the fire that was coming from behind the door. When he reached the door, he felt the door. It was hot to the touch. He reached out and felt the doorknob, it was also hot. He instantly knew there was a fire behind the door. Over the stage he could hear the sound of pandemonium. People were screaming and it sounded like a herd of elephants running towards the doors. He looked up and noticed that the fire was spreading from the room to the ceiling. Panic began to spread through his body, and he turned to run. He stopped himself, he knew that if he panicked it would not be a good thing. He took a couple of deep breaths and coughed, the smoke had started to flood the building, he looked up again and noticed that the ceiling was engulfed in flames. He had no time to lose, he needed to find Sara and get her to safety.

18

Jerry looked on in horror at the madhouse in front of him. He peered through the smoke and the blackness looking for Sara. The flames were growing larger as the cafeteria was being engulfed with fire. The front doors had been flung open as the sunlight from outside poured in causing it even harder to see. People were screaming and climbing over each other to get to the open doors. He noticed that bodies littered the floor, those who had been trampled while they were trying to escape the inferno that was blazing behind them. He carefully stepped over those that were on the floor, making sure not to step on them. He looked everywhere and could not see Sara. He made his way to the open doors while wondering why the policeman outside had not called the fire station yet. Smoke began to billow through the open doors as everyone inside rushed to get out. He tried to cover his nose and mouth with his jacket sleeve, but this did not work as well as he hoped. He pushed past a few others who were struggling to free themselves, looking back, he noticed that the cafeteria was fully engulfed in flames. The ceiling began to fall around them, trapping some between the burning ruins and the open doors. He wanted to help them, but there was no way without burning himself to a crisp in the process. As he exited the main doors, he moved to the side to get away from the burning building and the fleeing people. He bent down to catch his breath and clear the smoke from the lungs. When he stood up he looked around again trying to locate Sara, but he could see her anywhere. Then he saw someone running from behind the building. He got a quick glance of the person and he thought it looked like Homer. In the distance he could hear the sound of a fire engine as it approached the high school. He moved away from the building; the heat was starting to get to him. The person he saw running was heading for the library. He decided to follow him, moving swiftly towards the library, he caught a glimpse of the person as they went inside. Moving cautiously, he stayed close to the buildings, trying to move in the shadows so he would not be seen.

The sun was beginning to set, the blaze from the fire had spread from the cafeteria to the field that lay beyond, getting closer to the girl's gym. Jerry peered into the library ignoring the sounds of the approaching ambulances and firetrucks. It was dark inside except for what looked like a candle burning over by where the Civil War exhibit was placed. He could not see anyone, so he opened the door slowly. He knew that library was supposed to be open while the prom was happening, and that Mrs. Fredricks was going to be in charge of the book sale while the professor was doing some lectures on the exhibit. He slipped inside; all was quiet. He slowly made his way through the library and as he approached the counter, he thought he saw Mrs. Fredricks sitting at her desk. "Hello," he said. There was no answer. The closer he got to her, he noticed that something was wrong. "Mrs. Fredricks?" he said, again there was no answer. He walked up behind her and tapped her on the shoulder, her body fell out of the chair. Startled, he jumped back. He bent over her body and gently turned her to face him, his eyes widened, a lump jumped into his throat. Her throat had been cut from ear to ear, blood covered her shirt, her eyes wide open, her mouth in a grimace. He felt the air go out of his lungs; his stomach began to cramp up like it was tied in knots. He heard a sound coming from the direction of the Civil War display. He stood up quickly, making sure not to disturb her, he walked around her body. He moved as silently as possible to the other side of the library. As he approached, he stopped again, his eyes widened in shock. He could not believe the display of horror that stood in front of him. One of the round tables had a candle burning in the center of it. A tea tray with cups and tea pitcher sat next to the burning candle. It illuminated the grizzly display and Jerry thought he was going to throw up. Sitting around the table were the bodies of Doug, John, Sheila, Darla, and Mr. Payne. Their faces were pale, the expressions were one of shock, their clothes stained with blood. He backed up and turned away from the sight. Then he heard a voice come out of the darkness. "Beautiful, isn't it?" the voice said. Jerry looked around feverishly but could not see anyone. He continued to back up until he bumped into a table. He frantically turned to see what he bumped into when saw the display of muskets and pistols on the table. He remembered that the Aston Model 1842 was on this table, and there was ammunition for it there as well. "Don't worry about them," the voice continued, "they did not feel a thing, it all happened so quickly. But you, I am going to take my time with you." Jerry picked up the pistol from the table along with the glass box that held the metal balls. He smashed it on the table, and frantically picked up at least one of them. He did not know how to work the thing that he held in his hand. He knew it fired; he remembered the professor telling him how they had shot it before. If only he had asked him how to load it or even fire it. He decided that he would try to bluff without loading it. He held it up in front of him. "I have a gun." he said as loud as he could, "You just stay away from me Homer, or I will shoot you." There was the sound of laughter that seemed to echo around him. "I am not kidding asshole, you come close to me, and I swear I will shoot your head off!" He could feel the fear rise up in him, but he tried to stuff it back inside as he moved along the edge of the table. "You really think it is Homer. True, he is my son, and I warned Mr. Payne not to have this prom, if my son was not going to go, no one was going to go, but that bastard ignored me, so I had to take matters into my own hands. I decided to punish those who hurt my son." Jerry did not recognize the voice, could it really be Homer's father who had killed his friends, he thought. This did not make any sense. He continued to move along the table until he bumped into a person, he turned and looked, it was Detective Miller. He breathed a sigh of relief at the sight of the policeman. "The killer, he is in the library, he has to be over there I think." he pointed towards the table with the lit candle. Miller put his hand on Jerry's shoulder, "It's okay son." Jerry's eyes widened, he felt sick to his stomach, he tried to back away, but the man's grip was so tight. "You see, no one hurts my boy, he is my son, I could not let these people get away with it like that." He moved towards Jerry; his face was expressionless. Jerry held up the pistol again, putting it right into Miller's face. "I swear," Jerry said, "I will shoot you." Miller smiled. Outside the library, there was a bevy of activity. Firefighters were working to get the fire put out while paramedics were helping injured students and the facility. Police cars began to swarm the high school parking lot. Suddenly there was a shot from inside the library, it rang through the entire school, echoing like the sound of thunder, then all was quiet.

Epilogue

Dawn was breaking. Smoke hovered over the high school as firefighters began to wrap up their hoses and put them away. The cafeteria was burned to the ground along with the girl's gym and two other buildings. The aftermath of the fire was devastating. There were thirty people who were seriously injured, and ten that had died from either the fire or being trampled on while trying to escape the inferno. Police had discovered the grisly scene inside the library. Paramedics had removed the bodies and they were transported to the morgue. Sara stood in between the office and the library surveying everything. Her dress had torn, and she was shivering from the early morning cold that had spread over town like a blanket. She watched as the paramedics brought out Jerry and Detective Miller on stretchers. They were both dead. She overheard one policeman saying that Jerry had orchestrated the whole thing and when confronted by Miller, he killed him too before killing himself. She watched as they loaded them into the ambulance. A woman stepped up behind her and draped a blanket around her shoulders. She turned and looked; it was Mrs. Hollinsworth. She smiled down at Sara and put one arm around her. "It will be okay my daughter," she said, "We will find your brother soon."

Don't miss out!

Visit the website below and you can sign up to receive emails whenever Miles Cornelius publishes a new book. There's no charge and no obligation.

https://books2read.com/r/B-A-DDDX-JQPMC

BOOKS 2 READ

Connecting independent readers to independent writers.

Did you love *The Last Prom*? Then you should read *Blood City: A Misty Night Story*[1] by Miles Cornelius!

A serial killer is on the streets of Seatlle. Homicide Detevtive Grinder is trying to unravel the mystery and find the killer before he strikes again. Her new partner, Detective George Crossbones, is hot on the trail of the killer and is trying to stop him before he kills again. Will they be able to stop him in time? Time is running outfor the two detectives as they find more bodies and their suspects turn up missing.

1. https://books2read.com/u/mZ0lYR

2. https://books2read.com/u/mZ0lYR

About the Author

Cornelius James Walter Miles Cornelius is originally from Porterville California where he grew up. He attended Alta Vista Elementary school where he graduated in 1982. He attended Porterville High School from 1982-1986. In 1988 he moved to Oregon and joined the Navy in 1990 and was a cook for four years. In 2001 he went to college at Eastern Oregon University where he earned a bachelor's degree of Science in Liberal Studies with minors in Anthropology\Sociology and Health.